“Take it eas

“Why does **have to end with a fight when it comes to you and me?”**

“You know why,” Zoe responded. “It’s what we’ve always done.”

“It doesn’t have to continue this way.” Kyle met her gaze. “All I know is that I don’t want to fight with you. Instead, I’d rather be kissing you.”

Her eyes strayed to his lips.

“We’ve been in this room for over an hour now. I don’t know about you, but I’m tired of bickering,” he said softly.

She nodded, unable to speak.

Zoe made a small gasping sound of surprise when his mouth drifted across hers, and for a moment, she stiffened in his arms. Her fingers trembled against his chest.

Kyle pulled away and looked down at her, as if expecting Zoe to protest. When she didn’t, he took it as enough encouragement to deepen the kiss. As his lips touched hers once more, it was like oxygen to a fire that had been smoldering for years. The heat had overcome the ice and soon blazed into a wildfire.

Unstoppable.

Books by Jacquelin Thomas

Harlequin Kimani Romance

The Pastor's Woman
Teach Me Tonight
Chocolate Goodies
You and I
Case of Desire
Five Star Attraction
Five Star Temptation
Legal Attraction
Five Star Romance
Five Star Seduction
Styles of Seduction

JACQUELIN THOMAS

has published over forty-five books in the romance, women's fiction and young adult genres. When she is not writing, Jacquelin enjoys spending time with her family, decorating and shopping. Jacquelin can be reached at jacquelinthomas@yahoo.com. Visit her website, www.jacquelinthomas.net.

STYLES OF *Seduction*

JACQUELIN THOMAS

HARLEQUIN® KIMANI™ ROMANCE

Recycling programs for this product may not exist in your area.

ISBN-13: 978-0-373-86321-1

STYLES OF SEDUCTION

For questions and comments about the quality of this book, please contact us at CustomerService@Harlequin.com.

Printed in U.S.A.

Dear Reader,

You are cordially invited to attend the launch of the Spring/Summer collection of Roger Hamilton Designs. New York becomes fashion's playground two weeks out of the year—February and September. This much-anticipated event is the central backdrop for my story *Styles of Seduction.* Many of you were introduced to the Philadelphia branch of the Hamilton clan in my novel *Laws of Love. Styles of Seduction* introduces Kyle Hamilton and Zoe Sinclair, two people who are connected through their love of fashion design and the love they have for each other. However, they will have to learn that in loving someone, you give up a piece of yourself. I hope you will enjoy getting acquainted with this wonderful family and bearing witness to the marriage of love and fashion.

Best regards,

Jacquelin

Chapter 1

"This is the last one, Nelson," Kyle Hamilton announced as he carried a large brown carton through the door of his fifteenth-floor apartment.

His cousin rushed over to relieve him of his burden. "Thanks for letting me move in with you. If things work out the way I hope, you will only have a roommate for a couple of months at most."

Kyle wiped the perspiration from his forehead before saying, "Nelson, you don't have to be in a rush to move out. You're welcome to stay here as long as needed."

"You're sure I won't be in the way?" Nelson Hamilton asked. "Fashion Week is only a couple of weeks away. I know this is a busy time for you.

Mother has been driving her staff crazy for the past month getting ready for her show."

"That sounds like Aunt Vanessa," Kyle commented, a smile tugging at his lips. Vanessa Bonnard Hamilton was a renowned designer in her own right. She had worked briefly for Roger Hamilton Designs, his father's business, before branching out on her own to build the Bonnard couture label.

He navigated around a stack of moving boxes and into the kitchen, retrieved a couple of bottled waters from the fridge and strode back to the bedroom, where Nelson was unpacking one of the boxes.

He handed a bottle to his cousin. "I'm going to RHD for a couple of hours," Kyle announced. "I'm not completely satisfied with our collection. I want to go back over the final changes one more time."

Nelson unfolded a sweater. "I thought everything was ready to go."

"For the most part," Kyle confirmed. "But I keep feeling like something is missing. I always get this way when it comes to Fashion Week."

He walked over to the door. "I left some menus on the kitchen counter. The restaurants all deliver if you don't feel like going out."

Kyle was out the door before Nelson could respond.

He was happy sharing his huge three-bedroom

apartment with his cousin. Nelson had moved to Los Angeles a couple of years ago to try his hand at acting, but had returned home to Philadelphia over the summer. Since then he had been commuting to New York for auditions. It was Kyle who'd suggested that Nelson move to New York permanently.

Nelson had returned home to family drama between his mother and the rest of the Philadelphia branch of Hamiltons. Kyle and Nelson both thought it best that Nelson put some distance between himself and the tension.

While other New Yorkers enjoyed the Labor Day festivities, Kyle drove to the offices of Roger Hamilton Designs in historic SoHo, a trendy neighborhood in downtown Manhattan that attracted artists, retailers and businesses alike.

When he arrived, he turned off the alarm and locked the door behind him. All of the RHD employees were celebrating the Labor Day weekend, so he was alone. He insisted that everyone take the weekend off because he worked better when there were no other distractions.

Kyle removed a dress from its protective covering and laid it on the mahogany table in his large corner office. Examining it with a critical eye, he reached for a piece of sheer voile fabric lying nearby and fashioned it into a collar around the top of the dress.

Smiling in satisfaction, he pinned the material in place and then returned the dress to the garment bag. Kyle went through each piece, tweaking hemlines, changing or adding buttons or fabrics. The new spring/summer collection had to be a Fashion Week hit—Kyle would accept nothing less. The RHD fashion show would be the talk of the industry if he had anything to do with it.

At thirty-four years old, Kyle was the oldest son of Roger and Lila Hamilton. He fully expected to inherit RHD one day, so he worked hard to prove to his parents that he was worthy of the inheritance. His designs had received rave reviews for the past three seasons. He had even received the prestigious Designer of the Year award.

His paternal grandparents had owned a chain of dry-cleaning shops in Philadelphia. However, his father had chosen a different path. Roger had moved to New York and was soon recognized as a gifted designer. He met Lila Eustace soon after and she began working as a fit model for him. Within a few years, RHD became a huge success and his mother began designing, too. And Kyle intended to continue, and expand on, that success well into the future.

Shortly after 6:00 p.m., Kyle walked out of the building that housed the design firm. He was amused when he overheard the whispers of two women walking behind him. Women seemed to appreciate his six feet four inches of fit and toned physique, which he worked to maintain.

Whistling softly, Kyle unlocked his car and climbed inside. He would have dinner with his cousin if Nelson hadn't eaten already. He was thrilled to have a roommate—Nelson's presence would alleviate some of the emptiness he felt from time to time.

Kyle's mother often hinted that it was time for him to settle down. Kyle's mouth quirked with humor. There were times when he wondered what it would be like to have someone welcome him home, someone sweet and loving, but he refused to dwell on the thought for long. The reality was that Kyle was not husband material, and he had absolutely no desire to get married. His focus had to remain on his work.

"They've done it again! Our show is scheduled the day after RHD."

Zoe had listened to her boss complain for the past fifteen minutes about the day and time of his show, and it stirred a pool of irritation within her. "Jerry, it really doesn't matter when RHD's show is scheduled. Our new collection is brilliant." She softened her voice and added, "I just hope you're ready for all of the orders we're going to receive from stores around the world."

He released a short sigh and nodded. "I guess you're right."

Dressed in brown leather pants and a multicolored striped sweater, Jerry paced back and forth, fingering his goatee.

Zoe watched him for a moment, and then leaned back in her chair, arms folded. "When are you going to let this competition between you and Kyle end?" She had never met a man like Jerry Prentice. At times he seemed in control, but just the mention of Kyle Hamilton's name and Jerry could carry on for hours. As far as Zoe was concerned, it was childish.

It was common knowledge that Jerry and Kyle had a long history together. Their rivalry had started when they were studying design in college and grew more intense after they graduated. Kyle went to work at his family's company, while Jerry took a job at Guava International, RHD's biggest competitor.

"Kyle and I are not in competition," Jerry responded stiffly. "I just can't stand the man or his huge ego."

Zoe had her own issues where Kyle was concerned, but she was determined not to dwell on them. The preparations for Fashion Week had helped to keep her focus off the man who had toyed with her heart and then cast her aside with nothing more than a fleeting glance.

An image of Kyle rose in her mind, and for a second or two Zoe enjoyed the flash of heat whipping through her. However, the heat was soon replaced by cold fury. It was better for her to concentrate on that particular sentiment.

She pushed away from her desk and walked over to a rack of clothing. She pulled an outfit from it and said, "This is our showstopper, Jerry. It's your best work yet."

A huge grin spread across his face. "I agree."

"It's time you stop focusing on Kyle Hamilton. If you don't, you'll end up letting your hatred for him stifle your creativity."

"What about you?" Jerry asked. "Have you stopped thinking about him?"

Zoe made herself turn to face him and meet his gaze. "I don't know what you're talking about. Kyle was just my boss."

Jerry gazed at her but did not comment, so Zoe considered the subject closed, pulling a scarlet-colored gown off the rack and inspecting the fabric. "I think we should use more feathers around the top."

Jerry allowed her to change the direction of their conversation. "Hmm…let's spice it up a bit more with some tulle."

"And some polished gemstones," Zoe added.

He smiled and nodded in agreement.

Zoe's mind drifted back to Kyle Hamilton. She

understood why Jerry felt so threatened. What her boss considered arrogance was actually confidence emanating from Kyle's every pore. He was a creative genius. While Jerry was very talented, Kyle seemed to be in a league of his own.

She attempted to focus on the outfits hanging on the rack, but images of Kyle with his close-cropped dark hair, chocolate-brown eyes and sexy grin threatened to take up permanent residence in her mind.

"Zoe?"

"Huh?" She gave herself a mental shake. "I'm sorry, Jerry. My mind was somewhere else."

"Getting more creative inspiration," he responded. "I didn't mean to take you out of the zone."

"It's fine." Zoe picked up a sketch pad and made some changes to a drawing.

Jerry walked over to glimpse her adjustments. "Yes. I like that." He strode toward the door. "Take the sketch to the sewing room and give it to Martha when you're done. I want her to add the finishing touches right away."

Zoe did not look up from her work. She could hear Jerry shouting orders in the hallway. Fashion Week always seemed to make him more intense than usual.

When she was done, Zoe left her office with the dress and sketch in hand. She caught sight of a slender woman lurking nearby and sighed in irritation.

Zoe generally got along with everyone, and there were only a handful of people she simply did not like. Sasha Jones was one of those people. The woman made it her civic and professional duty to sniff out every ounce of gossip, making the rounds in Guava when she wasn't making Zoe miserable. For reasons Zoe could not fathom, Sasha had decided that Zoe was the enemy.

"I see that you're making more changes to that dress," Sasha said, gesturing to the gown. "What's wrong, sweetie? Are you second-guessing yourself?"

Zoe exhaled slowly before responding. Her patience was not limitless. Enough was enough. "I'm not having doubts about anything, Sasha. But I do hope you're not too disappointed that my designs were chosen to be featured this year."

For a moment, Sasha's eyes seemed to be caverns of ice.

Zoe bit back a smile as she stepped around Sasha and continued on to the sewing room. She had no idea why Jerry kept Sasha around. She seemed to do nothing more than find ways to stir up trouble.

There were more important things to think about, Zoe decided. She resolved to put Sasha completely out of her mind.

* * *

"Oooh, that witch," Sasha fumed. She hated everything about Zoe Sinclair. She especially resented the way Jerry fawned over the woman's designs. Sure, she had *some* talent—Sasha would give her that—but so did every other designer at Guava.

She was the one who had garnered all the attention until the wretched day Zoe had walked into their lives.

Zoe hadn't just taken the focus off Sasha—she had destroyed Sasha's relationship with Jerry. Sasha and Jerry had been lovers, but that had changed when he'd decided to become Zoe's mentor, much to her disdain.

Zoe was the one to blame.

Seething, Sasha brushed past a couple of her coworkers without speaking. She paused when she neared the sewing room, where Zoe was engaged in a conversation with a seamstress.

A fresh wave of hatred washed over Sasha as she spied on Zoe.

At five foot eight, Zoe was three inches taller than Sasha. Although most people considered Zoe beautiful, Sasha considered her plain, despite her smooth mocha complexion, dark hair and almond-shaped eyes.

Sasha ran her fingers through her long curly extensions. She was beautiful and she knew it. Like

Zoe, she dressed at the height of fashion, although she preferred earth tones while her nemesis wore more vibrant colors and large statement jewelry. Simple strands of gold or silver necklaces were more to Sasha's liking.

Zoe caught sight of her in the hallway. "Did you need something, Sasha?"

Her cheeks grew hot as she fumbled for an answer. "I…I was looking for Jerry."

"Why don't you try his office?" Zoe suggested. "It's located on the other side of the building."

Sasha scowled at Zoe in silence.

The seamstress wore an amused expression, which quickly disappeared when Sasha sent her a sharp glare before stalking off.

Zoe Sinclair was going to regret the day she ever walked through the doors of Guava International. Sasha would see to that personally.

Nelson was still settling into his bedroom when Kyle returned to the apartment.

"Sorry about abandoning you earlier," he said.

"It's cool," Nelson said as he put away a stack of folded shirts. "Having lived with my mother all those years, I understand how crazy it gets right before a big show."

Kyle sank down on the edge of the king-size bed. "Have you spoken to her since you left Philly?"

Nelson shook his head. "I still can't believe

what she did. You just don't do something like that to family."

Kyle knew Nelson was referring to Vanessa leaking the details of her husband's long-ago affair with his sister-in-law to the media. He had heard about it from Nelson's brother, Harper.

Harper had been so disgusted with his father's actions that he'd left the family-owned law firm and started his own company. He had recently opened a second office in New York.

"Have you eaten yet?" Kyle asked.

Nelson shook his head. "I wanted to get unpacked first. This room is really nice," Nelson told him. "Your apartment looks ready for the cover of a magazine. I still think you hired a decorator."

He laughed. "Actually, Bailey and Brianna gave me some decorating tips."

"When I get my own place, I will definitely have them come over to help me."

Kyle and Nelson left the apartment and made their way to a nearby restaurant.

"This place is a favorite of mine," Kyle announced when they were seated in one of the booths.

"I've heard that the food here is really good," Nelson responded as he picked up the menu. "A couple of friends recommended it when I was here last month for that audition."

"Have you heard anything back yet?" Kyle asked.

"Not since the second callback," Nelson said. "I have another audition in a couple of weeks. In the meantime, I need to find a job."

"Why don't you work for me?" Kyle suggested. "My assistant left for another position and I could use someone to take her place. The schedule is pretty flexible, except during Fashion Week, obviously."

Nelson broke into a grin. "Kyle, I really appreciate all you're doing for me. Man, this is great."

"I have to warn you that it's not all glitz and glamour, Nelson."

"I know," he replied. "I've seen enough of what goes on. I think it's why Mother never wanted any of us to get involved in the fashion industry."

"Then she's probably not going to be pleased that you're my assistant," Kyle said.

Nelson shrugged. "She no longer has any say about the choices I make for my life. Right now my mother needs to try to fix this mess she's created with the family. Family should always stick together."

Kyle couldn't agree more.

His cell phone rang, cutting into their conversation.

"Your phone's been blowing up for the past

fifteen minutes," Nelson commented as they ate. "That honey must really want to talk to you."

Kyle broke into a grin. "It's this girl I used to date. She's in town for Fashion Week and she wants to get together." He picked up his glass of water and took a long sip.

Nelson leaned back in his chair. "Let me guess... she's a model, right?"

"Actually, she's a painter," Kyle said. "I stopped dating models a year ago."

His cousin laughed. "You were always a ladies' man."

"Hey, I can't help that the women love me." Kyle wiped his mouth on the edge of his napkin.

"Still humble, I see," Nelson said with a chuckle.

Kyle leaned back in his chair. "You're just mad because Lena Swan picked me that summer you spent with us before we went off to college."

Grinning, Nelson shook his head. "I'm glad she chose you, Kyle. She was a strange female." He stuck a forkful of salmon into his mouth.

"I have to agree," Kyle said. "I didn't know what to do when she showed up one weekend with a wedding dress and rings."

Nelson howled with laughter. "That's what you get for lying to that girl, telling her that you were in love with her."

Kyle gave a slight shrug. "Lena cured me of declaring my love to anyone unless I really mean it."

Kyle had been through a number of relationships, but his brief romance with Lena had almost caused him physical harm—she had pulled a knife on him when he had broken up with her. His parents had finally been able to calm her down enough to take the knife. Lena's parents were called to come get her and were warned to keep her away from Kyle or the police would be contacted. Lena wisely kept her distance.

"I actually ran into Lena last year during Christmas," he told Nelson. "She proudly displayed her wedding ring and pregnant belly. She looked happy."

"Lucky for you," Nelson said. "Hey, whatever happened to that ballet dancer you were dating?"

"She joined Dance Theatre of Harlem and ended up falling in love with one of the dancers. She married him less than three months after we broke up." Kyle picked up a French fry and stuck it into his mouth.

"Ouch, that must have hurt."

Kyle shrugged in nonchalance. "It hurt my pride most of all. I cared a great deal for her, but I wasn't ready to be tied down. That was the problem with all of the women in my life—they all wanted to get married and have babies. I'm too much of a free spirit for that. It would stifle my creativity."

"You just haven't met the right woman yet," Nelson stated.

"I have to stay focused. RHD is going to be mine one day and I fully intend to take the company to the next level. In order to do that, I have to devote my life to it."

"So you plan to remain a bachelor for the rest of your life?"

"I don't know what the future holds, but right now my focus is on RHD. You know that when it's a family-owned business, people would rather believe that I was just handed my position. They don't want to consider how hard I've worked, but I don't care," Kyle said. "The naysayers in this industry only motivate me to work that much harder."

Even as Kyle declared his devotion to his work, he couldn't stop himself from thinking of the one woman who hadn't tried to force or manipulate him into a serious relationship.

Zoe Sinclair.

They had developed feelings toward each other shortly after she came to RHD as an intern, although Kyle never let those emotions bloom into anything more. From the first moment he'd set eyes on her, Kyle knew he had to do his best to put Zoe out of his mind. Deep down, there were times when he really missed working with her, but Kyle wholeheartedly believed it was for the best that she had chosen to leave RHD.

Because if she hadn't, there was no telling what might have happened between them.

And Zoe Sinclair was most definitely a distraction that Kyle did not need.

Chapter 2

Zoe settled onto the plush sofa in the living room and reached for the remote, desperate for something to distract her from the image of Kyle Hamilton in his signature black turtleneck and black jeans that had been at the forefront of her mind all day.

"Why can't I get you out of my head?" she whispered.

She counted every moment she had spent away from Kyle a blessing in disguise, but lately he seemed to consume her thoughts. It was probably because of all the media hype for Fashion Week. Plus, she was exhausted from all the long hours she was working, and her defenses were down. Her thoughts kept going in circles whenever it came to Kyle. Zoe needed to bottle up her feelings for him. She needed to be in control.

Zoe had left RHD five years ago and had not had any real contact with Kyle in almost a year outside of professional events. She and Kyle had not been on the best of terms when she'd left to work for Guava International. Although she would never admit it out loud, Zoe had loved her time with the Hamiltons. However, toward the end, she had decided it was best to leave and vowed to never look back.

It still irked her that Kyle had actually seemed relieved at the news of her leaving RHD. In fact, it downright angered Zoe. She had hoped he would plead with her to stay with the company, but he had said nothing. It was apparent that he didn't care if he ever saw her again.

She tried to shake the thought out of her mind, refusing to allow such memories to dampen her mood. Things were going well for her professionally. Several of her designs were being featured in Guava's show. She had worked hard to get to this point in her career.

If only I had someone special to share it with.

Zoe stopped surfing channels when she found the Fashion Channel. The host was interviewing a young designer whose first show was financed by a well-known liquor company. New designers were often dependent on sponsors when it came to runway events, but design houses like RHD and Guava could afford to finance their own shows.

Zoe was lucky to have a company like Guava behind her. Yes, she was very lucky. However, there were times when she wondered how things would have turned out if she had stayed at RHD.

A soft sigh escaped her lips. There was no way she could have stayed. Things were too intense between Kyle and her, and she did not like the woman she had become during that period in her life. Pining over a man who had rejected her—she had no choice but to seek employment elsewhere. She and Kyle had grown pretty close while working together, but after they'd shared a kiss, things had changed abruptly between them.

Now, looking back, she realized that leaving Kyle and RHD was probably the best decision she had ever made. It was hard working with the one man she desired but would never have. She had definitely made the right decision.

So why do I feel so sad?

"We are meeting with Cameron Childs and his event planner this afternoon," Kyle announced while going through his calendar. He and Nelson were in his office synchronizing their scheduled appointments. "After that, we will come back here.

My dad wants to meet with everyone regarding the show."

Nelson made notes on his iPhone as Kyle talked. "I met Cameron last year in Philly. He was attending a charity function hosted by Aunt Jeanette."

"He's cohosting the RHD party," Kyle announced. "We need to go by Lincoln Center so I can check out our backdrops. The tents are already up, so we need to make sure the set is completed correctly."

Nelson finished his notes. "I am going to check on the shipment of colognes that just came in. They're going into the gift bags, right?"

Kyle nodded. "You can give the cologne to the receptionist. She's going to put the bags together."

As Nelson left the office, Kyle picked up the telephone. "Mom, it's me."

"How are things going?" Lila inquired. "Is there anything I can do to help?"

"We've got everything under control. I'm calling to see if you'd like to have lunch with your son tomorrow."

"Honey, I'd love to have lunch with you."

He smiled. "Great. I'll call you later with the details after my meeting with Cameron."

"Oh, please tell him that I said hello," Lila requested.

"I will," Kyle promised. "Love you, Mom."

"I love you, too."

He ended the call and Nelson strolled back into his office. "Ready to leave?"

Kyle nodded and they headed out.

"Marissa sent me a picture of the baby," Nelson said, looking at his phone.

Marissa was the youngest child of Jacob and Jeanette Hamilton, and one of Kyle's favorite cousins. "Yeah, I got one, too. I can't believe she's married and a mother. I guess I shouldn't be surprised, though. Marissa always wanted to be a wife. Remember? It's all she used to talk about when she was little."

Nelson laughed. "Her dolls were always getting married. I think they had more wedding dresses than anything else. My mother even designed a couple for her."

"What about you? Have you thought about settling down?"

"Not really," Nelson said. "Right now I want to see if I can make it as an actor. I know my dad would have liked it if I had studied law, and my mother would have been happy if I'd become a designer. But I have no interest in doing either."

"You made the right decision to follow your heart, cousin."

"I believe I did."

They walked outside to a waiting town car. Nelson and Kyle got inside.

"Did you tell Aunt Vanessa that you're my assistant?"

"I did," Nelson said. "She's fine with it. I think my mom is hoping that I'll end up working in this industry full-time."

"It might not be a bad idea—at least until you can support yourself with acting."

"I'll give it some thought." Nelson stared out of the window at a billboard advertising Fashion Week. "It looks like the whole city is poised to become fashion's playground for the week."

"Yeah," Kyle said.

"My mom loves this hive of activity," Nelson said. "She thrives on events like this—fashion buyers, editors, paparazzi. This is her thing."

The car pulled into the driveway of the Childs Hotel and they got out.

They were met in the lobby by Roberta Dallard, the hotel event planner, who escorted them up to the restaurant.

Cameron Childs was already seated at a table near the front. He stood up as they neared the table. "Good afternoon, gentlemen."

He shook Kyle's hand first and then Nelson's. "I saw your mother last week," Cameron told him. "She's a very talented lady."

Nelson nodded in agreement. "Yes, she is."

They waited until Roberta took her seat before sitting down.

"I'll be seeing Harper in a couple of weeks."

"Is he coming to New York?" Nelson asked.

"I'm actually traveling to Philadelphia," Cameron said. "I have some business meetings lined up."

"I was wondering if my brother had planned to come to the city without letting me know."

"He wouldn't do that," Kyle interjected as he scanned the menu. "Harper never comes to New York without seeing the family."

"Roberta, can you give us an update on the preparations?" Cameron took a long sip of iced tea.

"Sure," she responded with a smile. "The tablecloths are here. I inspected each and every one personally. They are exactly as you ordered."

Kyle noted that Cameron appeared somewhat distracted, which was strange for the man who was a company sponsor and deeply involved with RHD's future. He silently wondered at the cause.

"Sounds like everything is on schedule," Kyle said after Roberta had finished and a waiter had taken their order. "My mom can relax now."

Cameron broke into a smile. "Lila's called me twice this week already."

"I'm not surprised," Kyle said. "She's a perfectionist—especially when it comes to stuff like this."

"Don't let him fool you," Nelson interjected. "Kyle is also a perfectionist."

Kyle couldn't deny it. "Roberta, please make sure that the florist delivers the centerpieces no earlier than an hour before the party. I don't want them sitting out any longer than that."

She nodded. "I'll give them a friendly reminder the day before the event."

He stole a glance at Cameron, who clearly wasn't listening to the conversation.

The waiter returned with their meals.

Kyle blessed his food before diving into his salad.

"I will email you the finalized menu," Roberta said. "Should I email a copy to your mother, as well?"

He nodded. "You can actually just send it to her. Lila Hamilton knows exactly what she wants when it comes to that."

When they'd finished eating, Roberta excused herself by saying, "I have a meeting in fifteen minutes, so I need to leave you all. Kyle, call me if you need to change anything."

"I don't think we'll have any changes," he said. "Thanks for your help, Roberta."

She smiled. "It was my pleasure."

After they shook hands with Cameron and Roberta and said their goodbyes, Nelson turned to Kyle. "Do you have that effect on *all* women?" he asked as they made their way to the elevator.

"I don't think Roberta even realized that I was in the room."

"What are you talking about?"

"You didn't even notice the way Roberta was looking at you." Nelson shook his head. "Or the way that she said the word *pleasure*."

Kyle gave a short laugh. "Coz, I think you're imagining things. Believe it or not, there are some women in the world who aren't interested in me."

He could think of one woman in particular.

"Yeah," Nelson retorted with a chuckle. "The ones who haven't met you yet."

Kyle still remembered the day Zoe had walked into RHD, excited about her role as an intern during her college years. His first impression of Zoe was that she seemed to have a chip on her shoulder. Her attitude didn't scare him, however. It was more of a turn-on. Had she been older, he might have considered pursuing her.

I wonder how things would have turned out if I hadn't been quite so noble.

The elevator doors slid open.

Kyle was shocked to see Zoe standing there. She wore tan slacks and a crisp white shirt that would have looked severe if not for the amethyst-and-silver choker and matching earrings she wore with it. She smelled divine and Kyle tried to disguise his deep inhalation as a regular breath.

Did I just dream her into reality?

They stood staring at each other for a moment. Well, he stared while Zoe glared at him.

Almost reluctantly, she stepped to the side to allow Kyle and Nelson entrance.

He cleared his throat. "Hello, Zoe. It's good to see you. It's been a while."

"It's nice to see you as well, Kyle."

She was polite, but the look in her eyes was remote. Things had been chilly between them since Zoe had left RHD five years ago. She had obviously been avoiding him since then, although he did not fully understand why.

"I see the years haven't removed that chip on your shoulder."

"Or made you any less arrogant," she retorted.

Nelson was watching them both. After a moment, he offered Zoe his hand. "I'm Nelson Hamilton. Kyle is my very *rude* cousin."

Shaking his hand, she awarded him a warm smile. "It's a pleasure to meet you."

Kyle suddenly felt an emptiness. There was a time when he'd felt that Zoe's smiles were reserved only for him. He stole a peek at her. She had turned her warmth up a notch and was beaming as she talked with Nelson. She did not spare him a glance.

"How long will you be staying in New York?" she asked Nelson.

"I actually live here now."

"The Big Apple is a great place to call home."

Nelson smiled at her. "I completely agree."

Kyle looked from one to the other. They were engaging in a full conversation and completely ignoring him. "How have you been?" he interjected.

Zoe glanced over at him as if she had just noticed he was standing there. "I'm great," she said coolly. "Couldn't be better."

She turned her attention back to Nelson. "I'm sure you know that there's a lot to do in New York…."

Did she just dismiss me? Kyle wondered when she turned her attention back to his cousin.

Kyle shook his head in disbelief. But he wasn't sure whether it was disbelief over her actions or the jealousy that he couldn't deny he was feeling as he watched Zoe Sinclair paying attention to someone else.

Part of Zoe's view was blocked by a muscled chest and brawny forearms beneath a black knit shirt, but she was determined to ignore his chocolate-brown eyes and the way sexiness oozed from his every pore.

The first time she'd met Kyle, he had made such an impression on her that Zoe had instantly responded with the eagerness of a teenage girl. However, that connection had short-circuited after the way he'd toyed with her heart.

"It's really nice to finally meet you, Nelson,"

she managed while making a determined effort to ignore the internal heat wave she felt. "I've heard a lot about you from Bailey. She talks about you all of the time."

He chuckled. "All good things, I hope."

Zoe smiled. "Bailey's said nothing but good things about you. By the way, I'm also a huge fan of your mother's designs. She's incredible."

Nelson broke into a grin. "She's indeed gifted."

Kyle nodded in agreement, but his eyes never left Zoe's face.

His intense gaze unnerved her, but she was not going to give Kyle the satisfaction of knowing he could still affect her in any way. She wanted him to see that he really did not exist in her world.

"So I hear you are very talented, as well," Nelson said.

"Fashion design is what I was born to do," she said. "I love it."

"What do you do for fun or when you are not in creative mode?"

"I rest," she said with a short chuckle. "Or my roommate and I check out new movies or we see a play on Broadway."

Kyle's eyes were sharp and assessing, but Zoe continued to ignore his presence.

"Perhaps you won't mind showing me around sometime," Nelson said smoothly.

"Sure," Zoe said.

She stole a peek at Kyle. His gaze glittered with anger. The tension between them was drawn so tight that Zoe half expected the lights to go out.

She tapped her foot softly on the floor, silently willing the elevator to the lobby. Zoe did not want to spend another minute with the man who had once crushed her heart without a care. Although she had grown what Zoe considered a New Yorker's hard shell, she was still affected by the hurt Kyle had inflicted upon her.

She glanced over at Nelson. She shouldn't have flirted with him like that, but Zoe wanted to see if it would bother Kyle.

Apparently it did.

"RHD is hosting a party on Wednesday," Kyle said, cutting through the heavy silence. "Why don't you come, Zoe? I know my parents would love to see you. Jerry's invited, as well."

"Only if you consider coming to Guava's cocktail party," Zoe said with a polite smile. "It's actually a couple of hours earlier than your event. Roberta mentioned it when we booked ours. And don't forget to bring your cousin," she couldn't help adding.

"Thank you for the invitation, but I'll need to check my schedule," he told her. "If I can make it, I'll definitely be there."

"I'm looking forward to it," Nelson interjected. "My schedule's clear."

She awarded him another smile. "Good. I'll be looking for you."

Zoe was pleased at the sullen expression on Kyle's face. It served him right after the way that he'd treated her.

Feeling his gaze on her, she pulled out her iPhone and scanned through her emails.

It won't be long before we reach the lobby. I just want to get out of here. I can't handle being this close to him.

After what seemed like an eternity in the elevator, the doors opened.

Zoe stepped out first, thrilled to be out of the confined space. Clearly Kyle still had the ability to make her weak at the knees, and the last thing she wanted to do was fall at his feet.

"It was nice seeing you both," she said coolly before walking briskly away.

She was angry with herself for inviting Kyle to the cocktail party, and for flirting with Nelson to make him jealous. She had often accused Jerry of being childish when it came to Kyle, but Zoe couldn't deny that she'd behaved in much the same way. It was just…wrong.

Kyle Hamilton seemed to bring out the worst in her.

But then again, Zoe already knew that.

Chapter 3

"What did you do to Zoe?" Nelson inquired as soon as she was out of hearing range. "She acted as if she couldn't bear to be around you." He chuckled. "I guess you were right—there is at least one woman who is immune to your charms."

Kyle was in no mood to laugh about Zoe Sinclair with his cousin. "She used to work for RHD, but Guava made her an offer she couldn't refuse. I don't think she really liked working for me."

Nelson shook his head. "I feel like there is something more between you two. I got the feeling that her interest in me was only to garner a reaction from you."

"No," Kyle insisted. "There's never been anything between me and Zoe."

He saw no need to mention that they had once shared a kiss one sultry night more than five years ago. Zoe's undeniable charm had been too much for him to ignore in a weakened moment.

"I don't know, man," Nelson said, looking as if he didn't completely believe Kyle. "There was just too much tension in that elevator. She wasn't fired, so what happened?"

Kyle shrugged. "I'm not sure. She's always had a chip on her shoulder."

"What's up with you?"

"Excuse me?"

Nelson repeated his question. "I've never seen you react this way around a woman."

"I don't know what you're talking about."

Kyle would never admit it, but seeing Zoe bat her eyelashes and flirt with Nelson had really bothered him. He wasn't sure if she was really interested in his cousin or if Nelson's suspicions were correct. Regardless, he did not like it one way or the other.

Zoe walked into her office and closed the door behind her. Her purse fell to the floor as she leaned against her desk, then sat. She closed her eyes as vivid images churned through her mind of her time at RHD working under Kyle.

There was a part of Zoe that wanted to hate Kyle for turning her world upside down with a scorching kiss and then acting as though nothing had ever happened between them, but the fact was there was much that she admired about him, such as his love for family. Although her Baltimore upbringing was not privileged in the way that Kyle's was, Zoe was raised by loving parents with whom she remained close. She had inherited her love of fashion from her mother. Some of Zoe's earliest memories were of playing in her parents' closet, trying on her mother's high heels and scarves. Her mom claimed that the first word Zoe ever spoke was *shoe.*

Zoe and her mother used to go shopping together almost every weekend as she got older. They never bought much because her parents made just enough money to make ends meet and had very little extra. Still it was fun trying on clothes and putting together outfits. By the time Zoe was in high school, she had started making her own clothes and earning extra money by designing for her friends.

When she was studying at FIT, Zoe devoured fashion magazines and articles on trends in the industry. Although she could not afford a subscription to *Women's Wear Daily,* she read every copy in FIT's library and kept abreast of the industry. That was how she heard about the RHD internship. Zoe had leaped at the chance to work for such a prominent design house.

From the moment she'd first walked through the doors of RHD, Zoe had felt as if she had finally arrived where she was meant to be. Like a sponge, she'd soaked up every detail of the business. Everyone at RHD worked hard, but Zoe worked harder. She was intent on proving her worth, and her efforts did not go unnoticed. There were three other FIT interns at RHD that semester—girls with sterling pedigrees and family connections—but Zoe was the only one who was offered a job upon graduation.

Most of Zoe's coworkers had embraced her from the beginning, praising her work ethic and her creativity, but Kyle had seemed unimpressed by her talent. He wasn't insulting or dismissive—he just accepted her accomplishments at face value. Zoe was determined to make Kyle Hamilton acknowledge her.

Maybe that was what led to tension between them.

By the time Zoe was twenty-three, her star was rising at RHD. Kyle had frequently requested Zoe for projects and Zoe took every opportunity to work closely with Kyle, despite their constant bickering. But working in such close proximity to the sensual designer had ignited a smoldering desire within Zoe that she didn't know how to handle.

Things had come to a head during Fashion Week 2008. After a successful show in Bryant

Park, Kyle had invited Zoe to join him and his friends at a party. She wasn't sure if it was the cosmos they were drinking or the excitement of the evening, but Kyle had kissed her.

Zoe had matched him kiss for kiss, each one more passionate than the last.

Abruptly, Kyle had pulled away, leaving her to try to figure out what had gone wrong. Her humiliation did not end there, however.

The next morning, Kyle pulled her into his office and apologized for crossing the boundary between employer and employee. To add insult to injury, he also had the nerve to say that she was too young for him.

She had to admit that the man was one incredible kisser, but the sting of his dismissal still felt as fresh as the day it had happened.

It bothered Zoe that she had been foolish enough to believe that Kyle Hamilton was tied to her destiny...and that she had allowed herself to fall in love with him.

Jerry stuck his head inside her office, interrupting her turbulent thoughts. "I have a lunch date. Can you review the list of candidates for Fashion Week internships? I sent them to you via email. We need a couple to start as soon as possible because two quit on us yesterday."

"Sure," Zoe said.

He was gone in a flash.

She leaned back in her chair and sighed. Zoe had a lot on her plate already, but she checked her email and found the list Jerry had sent.

When she came across one prospect who had interned at RHD last year, Zoe paused. She briefly wondered why the young man had decided not to go back there. It really did not matter, she told herself.

The important thing was for Zoe to put RHD, and Kyle Hamilton, out of her mind once and for all. She had bigger things to worry about than the man she had once been in love with.

"Have you seen Brianna or Bailey yet?" Kyle asked Nelson as they left his apartment for the weekly Sunday dinner hosted by his parents. "I know Daniel came by to see you a couple of days ago."

Nelson shook his head. "I talked to Bailey, but Brianna and I have been playing telephone tag. I'm really looking forward to seeing everyone."

They stepped inside a waiting elevator.

"Miss those family gatherings, huh?" Kyle asked as he pressed the button for the eighteenth floor. Kyle's whole family lived in separate apartments in the same building co-owned by Kyle's parents on Central Park West, which had its advantages, particularly when it came to getting together for Sunday dinner.

Nelson nodded. "I do. I enjoy being around family."

They rode three floors up and knocked on the door when they reached his parents' apartment. His mother rushed out to give Nelson a hug. "Welcome to New York."

He laughed. "Hello, Aunt Lila."

She slipped her arm through his. "I cooked some of your favorites."

Kyle followed them inside. "Don't spoil him, Mom."

Lila looked much younger than her fifty-eight years. Although she no longer modeled and had given birth to four children, she still maintained her slender figure. Today, she wore her long, dark hair in its natural kinky/curly state.

Lila looked up at her son and said, "Nelson's the guest of honor today. He deserves a little spoiling."

Kyle's youngest sister Bailey walked into the room. "We have been graced by a celebrity. How are you, cousin?"

Even in a pair of faded jeans and a black tank top with silver beading, the young model looked like a star, Kyle thought to himself. He had a strong feeling that this year's Fashion Week was going to launch Bailey's career, and Kyle was excited for her.

Nelson chuckled. "I'm no celebrity, that's for sure."

Kyle's other sister Brianna, a budding designer in her own right, joined them, followed by a man in his early sixties, bald with a salt-and-pepper beard and mustache. He pushed his designer eyeglasses up the bridge of his nose. "Nephew, it's good to see you. Although I thought you would've come to say hello before now."

"I'm sorry, Uncle Roger, I know how busy it's been for you all."

"There's always time for family."

Kyle sat down beside Nelson on the overstuffed sofa. "Family comes first—that's what my dad always says."

Roger gave Nelson a firm pat on the shoulder. "So you decided to venture on a different path than your father, I hear."

"Law is not in my blood. I think I inherited my mother's creative spirit instead."

"There's nothing wrong with that," Kyle interjected as Roger nodded in agreement.

"I wanted to be an actress once," Brianna confessed. "When I was twelve."

"Then she wanted to become an astronaut," Kyle's brother, Daniel, said as he came into the room with a chuckle. "But she changed her mind when she realized that the space suits were not fashionable."

Brianna laughed. "I figured I could just design

my own. When I found out that I couldn't, I decided that being an astronaut just wasn't for me.

"Kyle never wanted to be anything other than an RHD designer," Brianna continued. "I would be in my room designing clothes for my dolls and Kyle would try to change my drawings. It used to drive me crazy. That's why I bought him a doll one Christmas."

Nelson threw back his head and laughed.

"It's not that funny," Kyle muttered, before chuckling.

"I should thank you," Brianna said. "It's because of you that I am the person I am. You taught me a lot about designing."

Lila rose, checked her watch and announced, "Dinner is ready to be served. Shall we?"

Roger gave the blessing before they all ventured into the kitchen to prepare their plates.

"I'm really excited about the show," Bailey said once they were all seated around a table large enough to seat twenty. "I've got several interviews lined up already. I feel that this might be my big moment."

"I agree," Kyle interjected. "Since you appeared in that series of commercials Daniel created for RHD, you've garnered a lot of interest in the industry."

Nelson glanced over at Bailey. "You were so quiet and shy when we were growing up. I still can't get over how much you've changed. You, too, Daniel. You were always playing pranks or joking around. Now look at you."

"We used to have so much fun when we were younger," Daniel said. "Then we kind of drifted apart as we got older."

"We're going to change that," Nelson said. "Starting now. It's inspiring to be surrounded by such creative people. And you surround yourself with creatives, too. Like that woman you introduced me to today, Kyle."

Kyle looked up at his cousin and noted the twinkle in his eye.

"Who's that, Kyle?" Lila asked.

"I ran into Zoe Sinclair at the Childs Hotel," he announced, shooting Nelson a glare. "I was surprised to see her."

"How did she look?" Lila asked. "She was always so chic."

"Good," Kyle and Nelson answered in unison.

Bailey chuckled.

"I hear she's doing quite well over at Guava," Roger said.

"She's part of the reason their fall collection did so well," Brianna interjected. "*Women's Wear Daily* says that Zoe has a bright future as a designer."

Lila agreed. "We were lucky to have her for

the short time she worked at RHD. Wouldn't you agree, Kyle?"

Kyle nodded without saying anything.

"Let's go sit," Lila said as they finished their meal.

"Why did Zoe leave RHD?" Nelson asked when they'd settled in the family room. Kyle had been hoping they were done with the topic of Zoe, but Nelson didn't seem ready to let her go.

"Apparently she received a better offer from Guava," he replied, trying to keep his voice as neutral as possible.

"We should have fought to keep her," Lila said. "She worked under your supervision, Kyle. Why didn't you convince Zoe to stay?"

"She had already made up her mind, Mom."

"I think you underestimate your powers of persuasion."

Kyle met his mother's gaze. "Zoe is a grown woman. I'm sure she put a lot of thought into her decision to leave RHD. She's been with Guava for five years now, so it must be working out for her." When Kyle noticed his mother and Nelson exchanging a glance, he fought the temptation to leave the room.

"Did you and Zoe get a chance to talk about anything?" Lila inquired.

"Like what?" he asked, not enjoying where this conversation was heading one bit.

"Is she single?"

"We were only in the elevator for a few minutes, Mom. I didn't have enough time for a full dossier."

Kyle couldn't help wondering why his mother was always so interested in Zoe and her social life. Maybe it was because Lila knew Zoe was confident where it counted and independent to an extreme. Zoe wasn't afraid of going against the grain when it came to the achievement of her goals, much like his mother.

He had to admit that he admired those qualities in both women.

As Lila and his sisters gazed at him with a knowing look in their eyes, Kyle stopped trying to resist the urge to leave the room.

"I need something to drink," he said as he walked out, ignoring the soft laughter of his loving family, who clearly had no idea what was good for him—and what wasn't.

Chapter 4

"I saw Kyle at the Childs Hotel on Friday," Zoe told Jerry as they stared at some preliminary shots of Zoe's collection on her computer in her office. "He invited us to the RHD party."

"Did he, now," Jerry murmured. "I hope you reciprocated by inviting him to our cocktail party."

She nodded. "I did."

"Good."

Zoe gazed at Jerry. "Why are you two always trying to best the other? You're both very talented. Your work speaks for itself."

"I earned my reputation the hard way," Jerry said. "Kyle was born into his. He hasn't had to work for anything."

"Kyle's worked hard to earn the respect of the industry."

"Why are you defending him, Zoe?"

"I'm not," she said.

"If you say so," Jerry muttered.

It was clear to Zoe that Jerry truly believed Kyle had not really paid his dues, but there was no point in arguing, so she changed the subject.

"I've been playing around with an idea. Would you like to hear it?"

Jerry sat down in a nearby chair. "Sure."

"I was in SoHo over the weekend and I was inspired by the styles worn by shoppers from every country in the world—from chic to preppy to quirky. I was thinking we should create a SoHo fall collection with international flair."

Jerry broke into a grin. "I love it." After a moment, he said, "You know, I think we should attend the RHD party. How would you feel about being my date?"

Zoe paused a heartbeat before responding, "I'm fine with it."

He studied her face. "You sure?"

Gritting her teeth, Zoe lifted her chin and met his gaze. "Of course. Why wouldn't I be?"

"Are you worried about seeing everyone at RHD?"

Zoe shook her head. "No, it'll be fine. I'm looking forward to catching up with my former co-workers."

Her life was different now, she reminded herself. She was a woman on the rise, and Zoe would not allow her feelings for Kyle to get in the way.

All she had to do was keep her distance and things would be fine.

Sasha seethed with anger as she stood outside Zoe's office, eavesdropping on Zoe and Jerry deep in conversation.

"I hate her guts," she whispered. Sasha had never received an invitation to the RHD show in all of the years she had worked at Guava International. She had worked hard to earn a leadership role in the company, but it was to no avail.

She blamed Zoe for stealing the lead-designer position that should have rightfully been hers. After all, she'd had more experience and had been working at Guava four years longer than Zoe.

And she was pretty sure that Jerry harbored feelings for her nemesis, although he'd tried to convince Sasha that their breakup had nothing to do with Zoe.

She didn't believe him.

Zoe's invitation to the RHD party only added fuel to an already stoked fire. It did not matter that her enemy was a former employee—it only served as a reminder that Zoe was getting everything that Sasha desired.

"Some people get all the breaks," she muttered as she brushed past her coworker, "while others have to create their own opportunities." Sasha headed for the elevator that would carry her down to the cafeteria located on the first level.

What she needed now was some fresh air, lots of coffee…and a brilliant idea.

"Bailey's doing a great job," Nelson whispered.

Kyle agreed. As he stood in the greenroom, a feeling of pride washed over him as he watched his sister's interview for a fashion segment about RHD's show on a local news program covering Fashion Week.

He turned his attention back to his sister. "Micah Jones certainly looks intrigued."

"Why are you surprised?" Nelson asked. "Bailey's a very beautiful woman."

"Look at the way he's looking at her," Kyle uttered. "He can barely focus on the interview."

Nelson chuckled.

"Could you describe for our television audience what's going on backstage at a much-anticipated show like RHD's?" the host of the show asked.

Bailey smiled. "Well, as soon as we check in, we go to hair and makeup. If the models worked prior shows, the stylists have to basically erase any evidence of that and create RHD's concept. After that, we meet with the show's choreographer for a rehearsal. We don't get dressed until first looks are called—this happens minutes before the show begins so that the clothes are not damaged in any way."

"The camera loves her," Nelson commented.

Kyle couldn't agree more.

"I can imagine that it's pretty hectic backstage. How do you avoid putting on the wrong jewelry or grabbing the wrong pair of shoes?" the interviewer asked.

"We have dressers," Bailey explained. "Everything that we're modeling is on a rack labeled with our name and picture. The dressers make sure that our look matches the picture on their reference cards, including all of the accessories."

"It actually sounds very organized."

Bailey laughed. "It can be hectic at times."

"So then you're ready to strut your stuff on the runway?"

"Not quite," she said. "After we get dressed, a photographer takes pictures of us for the look book—it's a pictorial record of the show. We then line up in the order that we're walking. My mother usually says something inspirational to the models right before the music starts and the show begins."

"I've heard that some models have a preshow regimen. Do you have one?"

"I like to find an empty space to do my own private run-through. I just need some alone time right before a show."

When Bailey entered the greenroom ten minutes later, Kyle greeted her with a hug. "You did a great job."

"Really? I didn't sound like an idiot?"

"No," Kyle and Nelson replied in unison.

Bailey placed a trembling hand on her stomach. "I'm so glad that's over. Can we grab something to eat now? I'm starving."

Laughing, Kyle nodded. "C'mon. I'll take you any place you want. It's my treat."

Kyle felt confident that Fashion Week was going to belong to RHD. Between his designs, his mother's designs and Bailey's work on the runway, they would be the talk of town. It was the perfect way to raise his profile for the next step in his career. And then Kyle would have everything he'd ever wanted.

Except Zoe.

The thought caught him so off guard, he decided the best thing to do was pretend he hadn't had it at all.

After a long day, Zoe wanted nothing more than to take a shower and spend the rest of her evening in front of the television. However, she found that her roommate had other ideas when she arrived home.

"Why don't we go to Sushi Samba?" Liora suggested. "I'm in the mood for their miso-marinated Chilean sea bass."

Although Zoe didn't feel up to going back out, she was hungry and they hadn't had sushi in almost a month. "Let's go now, while I'm still standing," she said.

"Let me grab my purse."

A few minutes later, they were outside hailing a taxi.

Zoe scanned her menu as soon as they were seated. "I'm going to have the shishito."

"It's spicy," Liora warned. "I'm ordering the otsumami assortment. It comes with the shishito, if you want to try it."

They gave their drink and food orders to the waitress when she came to the table.

Liora leaned forward and said in a low voice, "The guy at the table on your right keeps staring at you."

Zoe stole a peek. He was handsome, and while she was flattered, she had no interest in even getting to know the man. The relationships she'd had were few and fleeting, leading to nothing but disappointment.

Kyle was a perfect example of that disappointment. "I don't think I can handle another letdown," Zoe stated. "I'd rather stay single."

The waitress returned with their drinks.

"Speaking of single, I saw your former boss earlier today," Liora said before taking a sip of her ice water. "He was with his sister and some guy at Ray's Restaurant this morning for breakfast."

"That was probably his cousin Nelson. He's working as Kyle's assistant. I saw them a couple of days ago."

"Have you ever considered dating Kyle? You do find him attractive, don't you?"

"He's handsome," Zoe acknowledged.

"He's talented and he's single."

"Right," she muttered.

"So why don't you go for it?"

Zoe didn't quite know how to answer. She'd met Liora shortly after starting her job with Guava and had never told her what had transpired between her and Kyle.

"Is he a serial killer?" Liora questioned.

Zoe gave a laugh, but it was without humor.

"Then what's keeping you from going for it?" Liora persisted as their food arrived.

"Liora, I wasn't his type," she explained after the waitress left. "We kissed once, and after that things were never the same between us. Kyle only saw me as his employee."

"Maybe he has a rule about dating coworkers," Liora suggested, sampling the edamame. "I can respect that."

"I can, too," Zoe said. "However, during the

time that I worked at RHD, I know he dated two different women he'd met on the job. They were models, of course."

"You work for Guava now," Liora reminded her.

Zoe wiped her mouth with the corner of her napkin. "The truth is that I don't think it would matter to Kyle one way or the other."

"Well, then he must be plain crazy."

Zoe gave a slight shrug. "I think he just wasn't in to me. He didn't kiss me until he was practically drunk."

"Like I said, he must be crazy," Liora stated. "It's his loss."

"I agree."

"So what do you think about his cousin?"

"He's handsome, but he's not really my type," Zoe said. "You should have seen his expression when I was talking to his cousin. I could tell he wasn't happy about it, but it shouldn't matter. He's not interested in me."

"I think he was jealous."

"I don't know, Liora," Zoe said. "He confuses me. Kyle doesn't want me and he doesn't want anyone else to be interested in me, either."

"Why don't you just tell Kyle to lay it all on the line," Liora said. "If he is interested in you, then he needs to tell you. If he's not, then he needs to stay out of your business."

Zoe nodded in agreement. "I really don't think

Kyle is interested in me. He just doesn't want me getting with Nelson. Not that I want to date his cousin."

"Give Nelson a chance," Liora encouraged. "Who knows? He may surprise you."

Zoe shook her head. "I don't know why, but I feel like I need to find a way to resolve these feelings I have for Kyle. I can't move on until I do."

"You two need to sit down and have a real conversation. I'm telling you—confront Kyle and you'll get your answer."

"I suppose you're right," Zoe said. "But to be honest, one rejection from him is more than enough. I really don't want to go through that again."

"How can you be so sure he's going to reject you?" Liora asked.

The thought startled Zoe. And suddenly she wasn't sure what she was more afraid of—that he would reject her, or that he wouldn't.

Chapter 5

Lincoln Center's Damrosch Park was buzzing with excitement. Huge white tents had been raised to house different events, and people were dashing every which way, getting the park ready for Fashion Week. Across the plaza, beyond the fountain, the streets were crowded with cars, and pedestrians leaped off the sidewalks and ran with complete abandon, trusting that drivers would somehow keep from running them down. Zoe switched her tote from one shoulder to the other as she made her way to the tent assigned to Guava International.

Her footsteps slowed.

"Are you kidding me?" she muttered softly.

In her path ahead was Kyle Hamilton. She'd run into Kyle *twice* in seven days.

For one panicked moment, Zoe wanted to dive behind a tree and hide until he was gone.

He glanced up, meeting her gaze.

Too late.

Zoe felt a jolt—like a current of electricity—rushing through her. The same jolt had passed between them on their first meeting. A wave of heat brought a flush to her cheeks and a tingling to her belly. She'd never had that kind of response to any man.

"Hello again," he said when she was closer.

"Hello," she responded.

Kyle watched her for what seemed like an endless moment. "Everything all set for Fashion Week?"

"We're ready," Zoe said as the heat intensified. Without thinking, she fanned herself with her right hand. "And you…I mean RHD…I'm sure your company has everything checked off?"

"Yeah, we're ready." He paused a moment before saying, "I hear you are taking over at Guava. Congratulations."

She gave a nervous laugh. "I don't know about taking over, but I do enjoy my work and Guava has presented me with a great opportunity as a lead designer."

"I'm really happy for you, Zoe."

She met Kyle's gaze, noting the sincerity in his expression. "Thank you. If it hadn't been for my time at RHD, I wouldn't have this chance."

"I don't know," he murmured. "A designer with your talent? You will make it anywhere you go."

Zoe chuckled. "A few years back, you felt quite differently about my work."

She waited for his response, holding her breath.

He broke into a slow smile before saying, "I always knew that you had talent."

Zoe was surprised by his words. She nervously pushed back a strand of dark hair.

"How's Nelson?" she inquired mischievously. "Has he settled in?"

"He's fine," he said. "Nelson's helping me out for Fashion Week, so he's going to be quite busy."

Her eyebrows rose the merest fraction. Was Kyle's comment meant to keep her away from Nelson?

"If you're not busy later, why don't you meet me for drinks?" Kyle suggested. "It's been a long time."

Whoa! Is he asking me out?

There was a time when Zoe would have been thrilled to receive such an invitation from Kyle, but that was no longer the case. The only reason he was asking her to have a drink with him was Nelson. He didn't want her getting close to his cousin.

"Zoe..." Kyle prompted.

Zoe felt herself begin to heat up again from the inside. "I have a really hectic schedule myself," she said, recovering her equilibrium. "There's still some preparation for the show. I'm sure you remember how much of a perfectionist I am."

"You don't have time for even one drink?"

"Sorry." Zoe tucked a strand of hair behind her ear again, this time with a hand that was shaking slightly. "I don't want to upset any of your girlfriends."

"That's the last thing you have to worry about, Zoe. I'm not involved with anyone. I haven't been for a while."

She fanned herself again.

"Are you okay?" he inquired.

"Yes, I'm fine," Zoe said quickly, and forced herself to look away. "I need to get going."

Kyle checked his watch. "Yeah, I need to be on my way, too. I guess I'll see you next week at the cocktail party."

She nodded.

"Perhaps we'll be able to have that drink then."

His low, amused laughter sent shivers rippling down Zoe's spine, and she forced herself to turn and walk away as fast as her Jimmy Choos would take her.

I did the right thing by turning him down, she decided when she had placed some distance between them. She was not going to allow Kyle to manipulate her.

But what if she was wrong? What if Kyle really was interested in her?

The question nagged at Zoe.

For one second, she thought about going after him.

Then she told herself to get a grip.

Back in his office, Kyle stared out the window. Zoe had turned him down flat.

Apparently the affection she'd once felt for him had evaporated. He decided that it was just his pride that was in shreds.

There was no way it could be his heart.

He could not deny that all he had to do was see Zoe to feel the same tug of heat that had caught him unaware when she'd first walked into RHD. The raw sexual attraction was new to him. Kyle had done his best to kill the flame but failed miserably. He was not going to give in to his desire for Zoe, however.

To prove it, he picked up the telephone.

"Roberta, this is Kyle Hamilton. If you're not busy later, I'd like to have dinner so that we can finalize all of the arrangements for the show."

"My schedule is open, so I'm all yours," she said.

Kyle recognized the seductive tone of her voice. He could not believe the way he was behaving. He was going to put himself through an evening of torment with a woman he was not interested in romantically, despite her best efforts, just to put some distance between him and Zoe?

Kyle pushed thoughts of Zoe to the back of his mind. He needed to focus on work.

Each time the telephone rang, he checked the caller ID, hoping to hear from one certain woman. Deep down, he knew that Zoe would never call him. Yet he continued to hold on to hope.

He was puzzled by his own actions. Kyle had never sat waiting for a woman to come to him. Zoe was different.

It was one of the qualities he liked about her, although he would never tell her so.

Several hours later, Roberta crossed and re-crossed her long, shapely legs, her high-heeled shoes bringing attention to her slender ankles. They were the kind of legs that could give a man some ideas, but Kyle was not about to pursue any of them.

"I have to confess that I was thrilled when you called me," Roberta said. "I had been thinking about giving you a call."

Kyle sipped his wine. "Really?"

"Yes," she said. "I've enjoyed working with you for the past three years. I feel like we've become good friends."

He agreed. "I think so, too."

Roberta reached over and covered his hand with

her own. "I'd like for us to become even better friends, Kyle."

"Everything takes time," he said quietly. "Right now my main focus is the show. I need to give it my full concentration."

She nodded in understanding. "Lucky for you, I'm a very patient woman."

Roberta Dallard was beautiful, with exotic green eyes. Her long, wavy blond hair was a gift from her biracial heritage. Kyle had noticed that she'd captured the attention of several men in the restaurant, and he began to wonder what was wrong with him.

There was a time when he would have quickly taken Roberta up on her offer, but his heart just wasn't in it. In some strange way, it seemed that Zoe had ruined him for another woman. Just thinking about her sent a warm sensation through him.

"Kyle," Roberta prompted. "What are you thinking about?"

"I'm sorry," he said. "I didn't mean to ignore you."

"I know you have a lot on your mind."

"I'm glad you were able to meet with me this evening," Kyle told her. "I appreciate all you've done for RHD."

"You make it sound as if we're never going to work together again."

"I don't mean it that way at all. I'm just distracted tonight. Shall we?" he said.

He paid the check and they left the restaurant.

A photographer standing outside snapped a photograph of them. There were several celebrities having dinner inside, so Kyle wasn't surprised to find media in the area.

"Why don't you come up for a drink?" Roberta suggested when he pulled up in front of her apartment. She gave him a seductive grin.

"Not tonight," he said. "I have a long day tomorrow."

"You're sure you don't want to come up?" she asked. "I could make you breakfast. I'm a very good cook."

"Maybe some other time."

"I'm going to hold you to that, Kyle Hamilton."

He got out of the car and walked to the passenger side to help Roberta out and escort her to her apartment.

"Thanks for tonight," she said. "I enjoyed myself."

"So did I," he said.

Roberta lifted her lips to his. Kyle gave her a chaste kiss, and then backed away. "Good night, Roberta."

"It could have been a great night."

"I'm sure." His smiled as he headed back to his car. Kyle did not doubt that an evening in her arms would be quite pleasurable, but he was no longer looking for one-night stands.

But he wasn't looking to get involved in a long-term relationship, either.

What did that say about him?

Kyle had to acknowledge that he really wasn't sure what he wanted. It was all because of Zoe.

"He is such a liar," Zoe exclaimed as she tossed the newspaper down on the glass breakfast table. Kyle had told her that he wasn't dating anyone. She should have known better than to believe anything he had to say.

"Who is?" Liora questioned. She drank a cup of coffee as she waited for her bagel to pop up from the toaster.

"Kyle," answered Zoe. "He *is* seeing someone. He asked me to have drinks with him a couple of days ago, but I'm sure it was only because I started asking him about Nelson."

"How do you know he's seeing someone?"

"Because I just saw a picture of him and Roberta Dallard in the *Post*," Zoe stated as she pushed away from the table. "Apparently they are the new golden couple."

"Really?" Liora walked over to the table and picked up the paper.

"I can't believe the lengths he'd go to make sure Nelson and I don't get together."

"But you don't want Nelson," Liora said. "Why are you so upset?"

Zoe leaned against the granite breakfast bar. "I'm not upset about Nelson. I just don't like the fact that Kyle tried to play me. I hate being manipulated."

"Maybe Kyle and Roberta aren't that serious. You know how things can get misconstrued, especially when it comes to rumors and gossip."

"I don't care who he's seeing," Zoe lied. "He just needs to leave me alone." The truth was that the thought of Kyle and Roberta together bothered her deeply.

"Have you gone through all of your invitations for the shows?" Liora inquired. "It used to be easy to get into a show, but now they are so overbooked and crowded. It kind of takes the fun out of attending."

Zoe nodded. "A couple of years ago, I could get extra invitations for friends, but I can't anymore. I'll give you the invites to the shows I won't be able to attend. With any luck, I might be able to get to one or two."

"I did get an invitation to a party to celebrate the opening of a new Illiana Sardi Designs boutique. You want to come with me?"

"When is the party?" Zoe asked.

"Saturday evening."

"Sure," she said. "There's a cocktail party a

couple of blocks away that night hosted by the Fashion Network. We can make a night of it."

"I'm looking forward to Fashion's Night Out," Liora said. "Last year I scored some great deals and lots of freebies."

"I know," Zoe murmured. "Jerry had us working late and I missed out on everything."

"Do you think you'll have your own label at Guava?" Liora inquired.

"No, I don't think so. When the time comes and I'm ready to strike out on my own, I'll have to leave Guava."

"You really should have your own label, Zoe. You already have a solid business plan and your designs are worthy of your name."

"I really appreciate your faith in me, Liora, but for now I enjoy the security of a steady paycheck." Zoe checked her watch. "I need to get out of here. Jerry will have a cow if I'm late."

"See you later," Liora said.

Zoe grabbed her purse and left the apartment.

As she hailed a taxi, the image of Kyle and Roberta in the *Post* came to mind. She felt anger heat her face.

She wanted nothing more to do with the man. In fact, she wanted to forget that she had ever heard of Kyle Hamilton.

Chapter 6

Kyle rotated his shoulders and tried to ignore the aches and pains from working all night. He had a very narrow window of about three hours, so he sent a text to Nelson stating that he was going to sleep and asked that no one disturb him.

Just as he was about to lie down on the couch in his office, his mother burst into the room. "What's going on between you and Roberta Dallard?" Lila questioned. "When did you two start seeing each other?"

He glanced at the clock on the wall, desperate not to lose a second of precious sleep time. "Mom, did you really just come in here to discuss my personal life?"

She folded her arms across her chest. "You didn't answer my question."

Kyle held back his amusement. "It was a working dinner and someone photographed us as we were leaving. Roberta and I are not dating."

"I hope she knows this, as well," Lila murmured as she moved to the window.

Roberta had called him earlier and invited him to her place for dinner, but Kyle was not interested. He intended to keep things professional between them.

"Mom, I thought you liked Roberta."

"She's a nice person," Lila said, turning around to face him.

"But you don't think that she's the woman for me."

"I don't."

Kyle laughed. "I'm not looking to settle down anytime soon. My focus is on my designs and carrying RHD forward into the future." He knew that Roberta was not the one he would settle down with. Kyle had not given much thought to marriage, but if he were to settle down, only one woman came to mind.

She smiled. "Your devotion to what your father has built is admirable, son. However, RHD will not keep you warm on cold winter nights."

The truth of her words prompted Kyle to remain silent.

"Your father and I don't want you to miss out. There is more to life than RHD."

"I know that," he said. "But I grew up in this place. I've worked in every department of RHD. It's in my blood, Mom. This is my life."

Lila placed a hand on Kyle's shoulder. "Don't you see, sweetie, that this is not the way it's supposed to be?"

"I'm fine with the way I'm living."

She released a soft sigh.

"Mom, you don't have to worry about me," Kyle assured her. "I have no regrets."

Even as he said the words, Kyle realized that they were not entirely true. He regretted the way he'd left things with Zoe all those years ago. But he decided it was best to keep that to himself.

The following week, Zoe was scheduled to meet with Roberta to finalize the details of the cocktail party at the Childs Hotel.

"Hey, can you take over some of the supplies for the party?" Jerry asked when she stopped by his office to check in. "Sasha and I will take the rest over after lunch."

"Sure," she said. "Are they packed up already?"

"One of the interns is working on that," he replied. He studied her for a moment. "Hey, what's going on with you? You don't seem like yourself today. Are you upset about something?"

"I'm fine," she said. "I just have a lot on my mind."

"I hope Sasha's not getting to you."

"She isn't," Zoe confirmed.

"Okay," he said. "Well, make sure that you're not late for your meeting. Roberta's schedule is pretty tight today."

"I won't be. I'm leaving in a few minutes."

Zoe was met outside her office by the intern, who was carrying a plastic crate. Ten minutes later, she was in a taxi and headed over to the hotel.

She arrived with just a few minutes to spare, and she decided she would drop the crate off in the supply room and then head to Roberta's office.

"Are you following me?" a familiar voice asked from behind her as she headed to the elevators.

This can't be happening.

Zoe turned around. "Maybe it's the other way around, Kyle."

"Regardless, it's good to see you again."

She glared at him, her stance combative. "Unfortunately, I can't say the same."

"Excuse me?"

"You heard me."

The doors to the elevator opened.

Zoe entered, followed by Kyle.

"Looks like you had the same idea as I did."

"What are you talking about?" she asked him.

His eyes traveled to the crate in her arms. "Are those supplies for your party?"

Zoe drew a deep breath; her gaze focused straight ahead.

Why can't this elevator move any quicker?

They stood in tense silence.

Zoe glanced down at her watch. She didn't have much time to spare before her meeting with the planner.

The doors to the elevator opened and she rushed out, nearly dropping the crate in her haste. She heard the steady rhythm of footsteps behind her.

Kyle seemed to be heading in the same direction.

Her mouth tightened when they stopped at the same supply room located down the hall from the ballrooms.

"I don't believe this," she muttered under her breath.

"Looks like we're going to be sharing this space," Kyle said.

Zoe rolled her eyes heavenward.

She walked briskly into the room to put away her crate. She was going to be late for her meeting if she didn't get going.

Zoe brushed past Kyle on her way back out, only to find that the door would not open. "It's locked."

"It can't be."

"You try it, then."

Kyle rattled the doorknob, trying to shake the door loose.

He turned to look at her.

"Like I said, Kyle...we're locked in."

"The door must have an automatic lock."

Zoe's eyes widened in a flash of anger. She rushed to the door and started pounding on it. "Help!" she called out. "We're locked inside!"

Kyle patted his pockets. "My cell phone must be in my car. Do you have yours?"

Zoe opened her purse and pulled out her iPhone. "I can't get a signal."

I can't believe that I'm actually stuck in a supply room with this man.

"Why is this happening to me?" she muttered.

"It could be worse," Kyle commented. "You could be in here alone."

Her arms folded across her chest, Zoe looked up and sent him a sharp glare. "I'd rather be in here all alone than with a liar like you."

What was wrong with this woman?

Kyle had no idea why she would call him a liar—he had not lied to her about anything.

"Zoe, I'm confused by the way you're acting." Kyle moderated his tone and tried for a more conciliatory approach. "Did I do something to upset you?"

Zoe ignored his question. "How could you just close the door like that?" she asked angrily.

"It's not my fault that we're locked in here," Kyle countered. "Neither one of us paid any attention to see if the door locked automatically."

Zoe was silent for a moment, and then she muttered, "I just want out of here."

"So do I," he said. It wasn't as if he was enjoying being in a locked room with a woman who treated him so coldly. Kyle searched his memory, trying to determine how or when he could have possibly offended her. The last time he saw Zoe, she was flirting with Nelson. Although she was not warm, she did not seem angry at Kyle.

"What's got you so upset?" Kyle asked her.

"There's no need to worry about me," Zoe sniped in response. "You should be more concerned about your girlfriend."

"What girlfriend are you referring to?" he asked, confused. "I don't have a girlfriend."

Zoe eyed him skeptically. "Then maybe you should tell Roberta Dallard that."

He gave a quick laugh. "You really shouldn't believe everything that you read in the newspaper, Zoe. Roberta is a lovely person, but we are nothing more than professional colleagues. She is not my type." It amused Kyle that she was jealous. "I didn't know you cared." He found Zoe intriguing.

"Don't flatter yourself," she said, that quick

flash of fire back under control. "I don't care who you're seeing. By the way, I always thought every woman was your type."

He was offended by her comment. "I am not a player or a womanizer, Zoe. I *do* have standards."

She did not respond.

Kyle leaned against the wall. "Every time I've run into you, I can't help noticing the chill in the air. Why is that?"

Zoe refused to look at him. "I don't know what you're talking about."

"Stop playing games, Zoe. You're angry with me for some reason. I deserve to know why."

She glared at him. "For the record, I don't care enough about you to be angry."

He drew back as if Zoe had struck him. "Wow...."

"I apologize for sounding so harsh. I just meant that—"

Kyle interrupted her. "Zoe, what did I do?"

Instead of giving him an answer, she walked over to the door and began beating on it again.

A few minutes passed. No help arrived.

Zoe released a long sigh in resignation as she sat down on the floor of the supply room.

Kyle eyed her for a moment. "Try to relax," he told her. "Someone will come. Unfortunately, we just have to wait."

Zoe's shoulders slumped as she tried her cell phone once more. "I still can't get a signal. I've never had problems getting a signal. This just can't be happening."

She looked as if she were about to burst into tears. Kyle wanted to comfort her but stayed where he was. The tension in the air was thick enough to slice.

He swallowed a sigh. *What did I do to make her so angry?*

Zoe finally broke the silence. "There was a time when I really wanted to impress you, Kyle. I wanted—no, needed—your approval, but instead, you made me feel as if I would never be good enough to make it as a designer."

He was surprised by her words. "It was not my intention to make you feel that way. You always seem to be in competition with me. I only wanted to remind you that you still had much to learn."

"I wanted to be the best," she said quietly.

"So did I," Kyle said. "And for the record, I've always been proud of you, Zoe. If we're being honest, I might as well admit that there was a time when I was somewhat threatened by your talent. I struggled with finding my muse during that time while the world itself seemed to inspire you."

Zoe looked surprised. "To me, it looked like your creativity flowed effortlessly."

Kyle noticed that her shoulders had relaxed, the anger lines around her mouth had vanished. She looked like the Zoe he used to know. She looked…

gorgeous. "Zoe," he began, his voice low. "I'm sorry for the way I acted after we kissed."

"That was a long time ago."

"That one kiss that we shared left an indelible imprint in my mind," Kyle confessed. "I know that I told you that we should forget it ever happened, but I can't. I remember not wanting the moment to end, but then reality set in."

"You suddenly remembered that I worked for you," Zoe interjected.

"Please let me explain," he said. "I felt guilty for putting you in a compromising situation. I just thought that if we stayed within our boundaries, things would go back to normal, but they didn't. You became so distant—I wasn't sure what to think."

"It was because of the way you treated me afterward," she told him. "Kyle, you dismissed me as if I was just another employee. You never once treated me like a woman with feelings. I was humiliated."

"I promise you that I will never make that mistake again, Zoe." His gaze slid over her. "One thing is for sure. You are definitely all woman."

Is it my imagination, or is it getting hot in here?

Zoe's face flushed with heat as she looked up at Kyle, watching him take her in slowly. He stood a few yards from her, pushing up his sleeves as if he, too, was suddenly feeling warm. Zoe couldn't resist a peek at his fabulous forearms.

Why am I being tortured this way?

She tore her gaze away from him, got up off the floor and walked to the back of the room, checking her phone. One bar of service came up. "I finally have a signal," she told Kyle, as she tried to make a call, "but it's not enough to get a call through."

Beads of perspiration formed on her forehead. If she didn't get away from Kyle Hamilton soon, she wasn't sure what was going to happen. "Jerry and Sasha were supposed to be coming with the rest of our supplies. They should have been here by now." She began fanning herself with her right hand again.

Kyle walked over to her. "Zoe, we're going to get out of here." He gently wiped the sweat from her brow.

She shrugged him off.

"Take it easy, sweetheart," he whispered. "Why does everything have to end in a fight when it comes to you and me?"

"You know why," Zoe said. "It's what we've always done."

Kyle met her gaze. "I don't want to fight with you. I'd rather be kissing you."

Her eyes strayed to his lips.

"We've been in this room for over an hour now.

I don't know about you, but I'm tired of bickering," he said softly.

Zoe made a small gasp of surprise when his mouth drifted across hers, and for a moment she stiffened in his arms, her fingers trembling against his chest.

Kyle pulled away and looked down at her as if expecting Zoe to protest. When she didn't, he seemed to take that as encouragement. As his lips touched hers once more, it was like oxygen to a fire that had been smoldering unseen for years. The heat had overcome the ice and blazed into a wildfire.

Unstoppable.

Chapter 7

Kyle's unexpected tenderness and the passion between them after so much time brought tears pouring down Zoe's face.

"Why are you crying?" Kyle asked her, confusion in his dark eyes.

"I'm fine," Zoe whispered. She did not add that she was blissfully more than just fine. For her, making love with Kyle was exactly as she had always imagined it would be. She would have told him that had they not heard voices on the other side of the door.

Zoe dressed quickly, spurred by the fear that someone would finally come to their aid and find them half naked.

Kyle buckled his belt as he called out for help.

"How did you two get locked up in this room?" the hotel worker asked when he opened the door.

If the worker had an inkling of what had transpired between them in that room, he was gentlemanly enough not to let on.

Zoe glanced down at her watch and groaned. "I have to go," she said as she rushed off.

Kyle caught up with her. "Zoe, don't you think we should talk about what just happened?"

"I can't right now. I'm already late." She felt the walls closing in on her.

"Calm down, sweetheart."

"I can't," she said. "Jerry is going to be livid."

"Zoe, it wasn't your fault. We were locked in the supply room."

She wasn't listening to him. "Maybe if I'm lucky I can still salvage this mess."

"Zoe—"

She shook her head. "I have to go."

Zoe rushed down the escalator, hoping the planner could pencil her in after she was a no-show for their appointment. She groaned again when she glimpsed Sasha leaving the special-events office.

"Where were you?" Sasha questioned.

"I got locked in the supply room somehow," Zoe said. "Where's Jerry?"

"He's back at the office. When I got here, you were nowhere to be found, so I met with the planner." Sasha broke into a wide grin. "Don't worry, I wrote down everything we discussed."

Zoe's smile was tight. "Thank you."

"Can you help me with these supplies?"

She nodded. "Sure."

Zoe struggled to keep from gritting her teeth. Sasha was the very last person she wanted to be indebted to…ever.

"It must have been very scary for you in that room."

"I was okay," Zoe said carefully.

"Really? How on earth did you remain so calm?" Sasha asked. "Especially being in there all alone. I probably would have freaked out."

Zoe was not about to tell Sasha that she had been locked in the room with Kyle. Her nemesis would run straight to Jerry with the news.

"Are you sure you're okay?"

She glanced over at Sasha and nodded. "I'm fine."

Kyle was in the hallway talking with the janitor when she and Sasha arrived at the supply room. Zoe glanced at the woman beside her and said, "I'm glad that you were here to take my place at the meeting."

"I am, too," Sasha said. "Jerry would be furious with you if I hadn't shown up when I did. Who knows… He might not have allowed you to keep your job."

"Why would I lose my job?" Zoe asked. "I was accidentally locked in a room with no way to get out."

Sasha nodded in Kyle's direction. "Looks like Kyle may be having some issues, as well."

"Why do you say that?" She glanced over at Kyle, who was with the custodian. They appeared to be examining the lock on the door.

"Why else would he be talking with the custodian?" She gave Zoe a sidelong glance. "You two weren't locked in the supply room together, were you?"

"As a matter of fact, we were," Zoe said truthfully. "Let's just get this stuff put away and get back to Guava." She put the bags she had been carrying on a shelf. "I thought Jerry was coming with you. That's what he told me."

"He had a change of plans," Sasha said. "It's a good thing, too."

Zoe held her temper in check. She was grateful to Sasha for stepping up, but she knew the woman would never let her forget it.

The question now, she thought, as Sasha looked at Kyle and the custodian, and then back at Zoe, was what else would she never let Zoe forget?

Kyle wanted to go after Zoe, but he decided to just let her leave. He would reach out to her later, when her overly curious coworker wasn't around.

Zoe had barely spared him a glance just now. He wondered if she had been able to make her appointment. Or maybe she'd just made up the appointment to get away from him.

He did not want to consider that possibility. Especially not after the way they had just made love. He had no idea how they had gotten locked in that room, but after what they'd shared, Kyle had no regrets.

Zoe had feelings for him—that much Kyle was sure of—but he knew instinctively that she wasn't ready to admit it.

The truth was that he also cared for her.

He couldn't deny that any longer.

When he returned to his office thirty minutes later, Kyle picked up the phone.

Her voice mail came on.

"Hey, it's me. I wanted to check on you. Give me a call when you get this message. Zoe, I really want to talk to you."

He hung up, frustrated that he couldn't talk to her right away. The connection he'd felt from the moment he'd first laid eyes on Zoe was still there. Kyle did not know what it all meant, but he did know one thing: he longed to possess Zoe heart and soul. He had never felt this way about anybody.

He was conflicted over his feelings because allowing himself to get close to her meant giving up a part of his own soul. But Zoe had gotten under his skin and he knew with every fiber of his being that there would be no other woman for him.

Zoe rested her forehead against the beige ceramic tiles while hot, pulsing streams of water pounded against her back.

"What was I thinking?" she whispered.

How could she give herself so freely to the man she loved but knew without a doubt did not love her in return?

Out of the shower, Zoe dried off and dressed in a pair of pink sweats and a tank top. As she sat on her bed and tried to figure out her next move, her cell phone rang.

She was surprised to see Kyle's number on caller ID but could not bring herself to answer, because she'd just proved that when it came to Kyle Hamilton, she could not control herself.

She was sure that for Kyle, what had happened between them in the room had been no more than an instinctive male response to a situation already charged with tension.

To add to her humiliation, Sasha had had to take her place at the meeting. Zoe had assumed that she would go running to Jerry as soon as they returned to the office, but he never said anything. Zoe figured that meant that Sasha was waiting for a more opportune moment.

Best to tell Jerry about what had happened in

the morning, Zoe decided, so Sasha would not be able to hold anything over her head.

Zoe left her bedroom and went to greet her roommate, who had just come in. "Hey, Liora. I was just about to order some dinner. Are you hungry?"

"I'm in the mood for Thai," Liora said with a tired smile. "Girl, that little pop star Jerri Bell worked my nerves today. She kept messing up her makeup and then yelling at me to fix it like I was her personal maid."

Zoe laughed. "I hear that she is a bit of a diva. Jerry designed her gown for the Grammys and vowed to never work with her again."

"I can certainly understand why he feels that way." Liora set her work bag down on the floor in the living room.

"I'll order dinner," Zoe said.

"How was your day?" Liora asked when Zoe hung up the phone.

"It was interesting," Zoe said. "Kyle and I got locked in the supply room at the Childs Hotel for over an hour. I was then late for my meeting and Sasha, of all people, bailed me out."

"You're kidding me."

"I wish I was," Zoe said as she went to answer the door and pay the deliveryman. "Sadly, it's all very true."

"So what did you and Kyle talk about while you

were locked together in that room all that time?" Liora asked as she pulled out some plates for their takeout.

"He told me that he and Roberta Dallard are not a couple."

"Do you believe him?"

"I guess so," Zoe replied. "He has no reason to lie about something like that to me."

Liora studied her for a moment. "Did something else happen between you and Kyle?"

"Not really," Zoe said. She wasn't ready to talk about what had transpired between her and Kyle. She was still trying to get used to reality of what had happened.

Liora watched her for a moment, and then changed the subject. "I'm so excited about working the Guava show with you this year."

"After your work was featured in *Glamour*, Jerry was more than happy to use your artistry on our models."

"Fashion Week starts on Thursday," Liora said. "Can you believe that it's here already? I'm looking forward to Vanessa Bonnard's pregala on Tuesday night."

Zoe felt her face heat up at the very thought of seeing Kyle again, but it was unavoidable and she'd better get used to it. They would be running into each other frequently over the next week.

"Are you listening to me?" Liora asked.

She nodded. “I’ve just got a lot on my mind right now.”

“What’s going on with you, Zoe? Are you feeling anxious about the show?”

“Somewhat,” she said. “I’ll be fine after a good night’s sleep.”

“Drink a cup of herbal tea,” Liora suggested. “It should help calm you.”

“I will.”

Liora helped Zoe clean up after they finished eating. Zoe could feel her roommate watching her closely.

“You never did tell me what happened with Kyle while you two were locked up all that time,” Liora finally said.

“We talked about Roberta and why I left RHD.”

“How did it go?”

“I don’t think that anything was resolved,” Zoe replied honestly, stifling a yawn. “I’m sorry, Liora. I must be more exhausted than I thought. I’m going to call it a night.”

“I won’t be long behind you,” her roommate said.

Zoe walked into her bedroom and climbed into the king-size bed. She propped up the pillows against the fabric headboard and lay back. She kept wishing that she could wake up from this dream.

There was just one problem.

It was no dream.

Zoe squeezed her eyes shut in an attempt to block out the image of her and Kyle making love without any thought that someone could have walked in on them. Worse, what if Sasha had found them? Jerry would have been livid.

More than that, she wondered what Kyle thought about their making love. Were his thoughts just as turbulent as her own?

Chapter 8

Kyle checked his phone—again—to see if Zoe had returned his call.

"You must be expecting an important phone call," Nelson commented.

"I thought I'd hear from someone tonight, but I guess not." He set his phone down on the coffee table where a small mountain of personal correspondence waited for his attention. Kyle picked up the first envelope in the stack.

"I can't believe you and Zoe were locked inside that room for all that time," Nelson said.

"The strange thing about it is that someone had to have locked us in, according to the custodian," Kyle stated, tapping the envelope against his desk. "The door didn't lock on its own."

"What do you think happened?"

He gave a slight shrug. "I guess someone mistakenly locked the door. It's the only thing that makes sense."

Nelson chuckled. "It was fate."

"It wasn't the worst thing that could've happened, I have to admit. Zoe and I were able to have a real conversation. Something that was long overdue."

"Good," Nelson said. "Maybe the next time I see Zoe, the air won't be so thick with tension. I could've cut it with a knife the last time we were all together."

"I don't think you have to worry about that. I think we are finally in a good space. We still have to work some things out, but I'm sure we'll get there."

Deep down, Kyle wondered why Zoe had not bothered to call him back. She could be busy at work, he reasoned. It was Fashion Week, after all. No one knew better than he did what that meant.

He just needed to relax.

Zoe would call him whenever she was ready to talk. At least he hoped that she would. There was much that Kyle wanted to say to her.

"I'm going to work on my audition," Nelson announced. "Are you planning to be up for a while?"

He nodded. "I'm going to have a glass of wine and maybe watch some television."

"Daniel said he might drop by for drinks later."

Kyle chuckled. "Don't count on seeing my brother until he actually shows up. He'll get home and fall asleep in a minute."

Nelson laughed and went to his room, and Kyle turned his attention back to the mail on his desk. Reading through a bunch of correspondence was the last thing on his mind. All he wanted to do was talk to Zoe.

Kyle muttered a curse. Zoe shouldn't be able to affect him like this...despite the fact that the moment he'd touched her, she had ignited an everlasting flame in him.

I'd better get a grip on my hormones.

He checked his phone once more.

Shaking his head in confusion, Kyle returned his attention to the task at hand.

"This is some party," Liora murmured as she and Zoe entered the huge ballroom at the Ritz-Carlton where the magazine *Focus* was hosting a party.

Zoe smiled at her roommate. "Wait until we get to the bash sponsored by Vanessa Bonnard. Nelson will be there, so you'll get to meet him."

"What are you going to do when Kyle shows up?" Liora asked.

"I'll simply say hello and keep it moving," she said with a tight smile.

"Zoe, you are crazy about this man. If you don't warm up to him—and soon—he just might end up with someone else for real."

She met Liora's gaze. "Just because I have feelings for him doesn't mean that he feels the same way. Remember, I've been through this before with Kyle. I'm not going to give him another opportunity to hurt me."

"You can't keep living in the past, Zoe."

"I agree, but I also don't need to keep making the same mistakes over and over again."

They left the cocktail party shortly after eight and headed over to the NoMad Hotel, where Vanessa Bonnard's rooftop party was in full swing. Vanessa glided around the room dressed in a bright green sheer top with a black tube top underneath and wide-leg black pants.

Zoe noted that every guest in attendance seemed to be toasting, air-kissing and posing for pictures.

"I love this place," Liora said loudly, trying to compete with the music playing in the background. "I hate that it'll be closed after Fashion Week until next summer."

"The rooftop dining room is one of my favorites, as well. Actually, Kyle brought me here when I started at RHD."

Looking back, Zoe had the sudden realization that Kyle had been trying to impress her. He had accurately guessed that she had never been inside a luxury hotel like the NoMad. It had worked like a charm—Kyle had made her feel special. He had also introduced her to a world she had never known—a glamorous world of celebrity parties that drew the crème de la crème of New York and Hollywood.

Zoe felt Kyle's presence before she laid eyes on him. She turned around and found him standing a few yards away from her, talking to his aunt. Their gazes met and held.

She broke the connection.

"He's here," she said to Liora, leading her friend away, over to the bar, where she ordered a white-chocolate martini.

"You can't hide behind that drink, Zoe. Go talk to Kyle. You know that you want to. . . ."

"Maybe later," Zoe lied. She had no intention of approaching him. It was too soon for her.

Maybe after two or three martinis.

Her eyes traveled the room as she looked for Nelson. She found him near the bar talking to his father. She recognized Vanessa Bonnard's husband from a photo in *Eminence* magazine last year. He seemed to prefer to stay out of the spotlight when it came to his wife's career.

Her eyes traveled to Kyle as Liora moved away to speak to Nelson.

Zoe smiled tentatively as he approached, and

then reached to tuck a curly strand of hair behind her ear. He was near enough for the warmth of his body to reach out and touch her, taking her by surprise. Her only escape was to take a step back.

Even after Kyle reached her side, he couldn't seem to stop looking at her.

He leaned over and whispered in her ear, "You never called me back."

"I know," she murmured. How could she put into words what had taken place between them and her feelings afterward? "I wasn't ready to talk about what happened."

Well, so much for staying away from him. Zoe sighed, despising her weakness. She should have walked away when she saw him coming toward her. It was too late now.

"I want you to know that I don't regret what we shared."

She glanced up at him. "You don't?"

Kyle shook his head.

"What about you?" he asked. "Do you regret what happened?"

"This is not the time or place to have this discussion," she responded.

"This is quite a party," Zoe said after a moment, as they watched a couple on the dance floor.

"It is." Kyle gestured toward the double doors. "Look who just walked in."

Zoe followed his gaze. "Benito Valentine." She

admired the way the up-and-coming designer had mixed bright earth-tone-colored dresses and vintage-inspired blazers at his fall presentation. She'd met him a few months ago at an industry networking event and found him to be warm and friendly.

Benito's date was in a gorgeous Benito-original retro dress in bright orange. Zoe herself had chosen to wear a black-and-fuchsia dress designed by their host. Jerry would probably be fuming to see her in a Vanessa Bonnard original, but she did not care. Tonight was about her—it had nothing to do with Guava.

"My aunt's designs look stunning on you," Kyle complimented her.

"I do love her collections," she admitted.

Zoe tipped her glass, swallowing the last decadent drops of white-chocolate martini. She needed all the strength she could get right now.

"Why don't we get something to eat?" Kyle suggested. He turned to accept a cocktail from an approaching waiter.

They walked past an actress being interviewed by a member of the press, saying, "Fashion Week is wonderful because it's a departure from what I do...."

Zoe glanced over at Kyle and smiled. "Didn't you have a picture of her in your office?"

He nodded. "That was a long time ago. It's not

there anymore." He tossed back a swallow of his drink.

"Why not?" she asked him. "If I remember correctly, you had a huge crush on her."

Kyle laughed. "Why would you remember something like that?"

Zoe shrugged in nonchalance. "I guess it just reminded me of how my brother used to have posters of actresses all over his wall. He seemed to have a different crush every week."

"Okay, so who was your celebrity crush?" Kyle questioned. "Was it Denzel Washington?"

"Nope."

"Okay…then it must be Blair Underwood." Kyle downed the rest of his glass in one swallow.

Laughing, Zoe shook her head. "I don't have one, Kyle. I was more in love with fashion magazines and fiction growing up." She handed her empty martini glass to a passing server, and then they caught up with Nelson and Liora in the buffet line.

"I see that you two have already met," Kyle said.

"My mother introduced us," Nelson said with a smile. "Liora has worked several of her shows."

They sat down together at a nearby table.

Zoe could feel Kyle's gaze on her. She tried to ignore the rush of heat she felt just being close to him again. She definitely wasn't about to acknowledge the stutter of her heartbeat or the tingling in her belly.

"Would you like to dance?" he asked.

"Sure."

Kyle took Zoe by the hand, leading her to the dance floor.

On the dance floor, her skin hummed from the contact with him. Zoe struggled with maintaining her rhythm while dealing with her knees wobbling over the intensity of his gaze.

When the music slowed, she took it as her cue to say, "I think I need a glass of water." Zoe was not sure she could handle the feel of his strong arms holding her close as they matched the slow tempo of the music.

Kyle escorted her back to the table, and then left to get a glass of water for her.

"You two looked good out there," Liora told her when she sat down beside Zoe. "I don't know where you got the impression that this man isn't interested in you. From where I'm sitting, I would say that he is definitely attracted to you."

She feigned nonchalance. "I'm not going to hold my breath on that one, Liora. I thought the same thing when I worked at RHD only to have him prove me wrong. I'm not going through that ever again."

The words sounded good coming out of her mouth, but did she have the strength to stick to them? The fact was, she loved Kyle as much today as she did back then.

She was treading through dangerous territory, she silently acknowledged. However, she would never be so careless with her heart.

Kyle was surprised when Zoe checked her watch and then rose to her feet. "I'm going to have to call it a night."

"You're leaving now?" Kyle asked.

"It's getting really late and I have to be at work early. I need to take care of some last-minute details before opening day. I'm sure you of all people can understand."

He nodded. "At some point, we really need to carve out some time to talk, Zoe."

"Kyle, what happened between us…it was a mistake. Let's just leave it at that."

Kyle took a deep breath and exhaled slowly. He couldn't believe what he was hearing. Was Zoe actually trying to say that she regretted being with him? That just wasn't possible. She wanted him as much as he wanted her. He could feel it. And right now he just wanted to keep her close to him.

"I don't agree," he said. "What we shared was special."

"Keep your voice down, please," Zoe demanded, frowning.

He eyed her. "What's going on with you? I

thought we had a great time tonight. Why are you acting this way?"

She blew out a breath and tightened the death grip she had on the strap of her clutch. "Because I don't want to have this conversation right now," Zoe said. "This is not the time or the place."

"Then give me a better time and place," Kyle urged.

Zoe glanced around. "It will happen when it's supposed to—that's all I can say for now."

He watched as, head held high, Zoe walked quickly away.

"If I didn't know any better, I would say that Zoe is running from me," he told Nelson as he sat down next to his cousin.

"I thought things were better between you two."

"I thought so, too, but apparently I was wrong."

Yet he could not forget the way Zoe's big brown eyes smoked with heat, sending out an unspoken message when they'd made love. Apparently she was as incapable as he of resisting the attraction between them.

"Where's Zoe?" his sister Bailey asked when she sat down beside Kyle at one of the tables near the dance floor.

"She had to leave."

"Oh, I hate that. I wanted to talk to her."

So did I, Kyle thought.

"Did you invite her to the show?"

"I didn't specifically," he said. "But I'm sure she received an invite. She's gotten one every year." Kyle was pretty sure that was his mother's handiwork.

Bailey eyed him. "You okay?"

He nodded.

"Good. How would you like to dance with your sister?"

Kyle looped his arm through hers. "I'd be honored."

As he led his sister to the dance floor, he couldn't help remembering the feel of Zoe in his arms. He had to talk to her about what had happened.

And next time, he'd do it privately.

Chapter 9

The sun was streaming into the apartment, matching Zoe's mood. She had slept well and was up early to get her day started. Tonight was the Guava cocktail party and they had an impressive list of VIPs attending, including the top bestselling R & B and hip-hop artists and a few Hollywood A-listers, as well.

"Wow, you're in a good mood this morning," Liora observed as Zoe practically bounded into the kitchen. "I need some of what you had. Right now I just want to crawl back into my bed."

"I'm just excited about this week," she exclaimed. "I feel like something big is going to happen."

Kyle had nothing to do with her sunny disposition. She had enjoyed seeing him last night, but the evening had ended on a bit of a sour note. He was insistent on discussing what had happened between them while she preferred to just forget her moment of insanity.

Kyle had shaken her more than she cared to admit.

He was planning to attend the party tonight, and Zoe had mixed feelings about seeing him. Just being near him had awakened emotions Zoe had trained herself to ignore. They were back in full force and she was not sure how to handle them. The truth was that she hadn't had any experience with this sort of thing.

Kyle was her first and only love.

The few men she'd dated since leaving RHD had not come close to affecting her the way that Kyle had.

Zoe pulled her attention back to Liora, who was pouring herself a cup of coffee. "I'll see you at the Guava party tonight?"

"Definitely. I wouldn't miss it. As long as this caffeine does what it's supposed to do."

Zoe said goodbye to her roommate and headed to work, but she still couldn't concentrate, even once she'd arrived at the office, which was buzzing with an insane amount of activity as people worked to get ready for the cocktail party that night. Time and again, her thoughts returned to Kyle.

His face.

His chocolate-brown gaze fixed on her as if Kyle could see straight through her.

His lips. Just the caress of those lips on her mouth the other day had set her body aflame.

She quickly reminded herself of Kyle's cool dismissal after their first kiss and of the humiliation she'd felt afterward.

She could not let go of that memory—it was the only way to protect her heart.

And it was clear to her now that she had to protect her heart at all costs.

Kyle walked into the Briar Ballroom expectantly. He could only spend a few minutes with Zoe before he had to make his way upstairs to the RHD party.

As soon as he entered the room, his gaze landed on her. She hadn't seen him yet, which gave him a chance to observe her—every gorgeous inch of her.

Zoe was a woman comfortable with her body, every movement easy and fluid. Kyle had heard people talk about time standing still, but until he'd looked into those beautiful eyes—even from across the room, her eyes made him forget everything else—he hadn't known what they meant.

But he definitely did now.

All Kyle could focus on was Zoe.

And then she saw him.

Zoe walked toward him in a perfect dress, her eyes wide and hesitant. Her vulnerability only heightened the attraction Kyle felt.

"Wow," Kyle uttered.

She gave him a gracious smile.

He drew in a breath that carried her sensual fragrance. His gaze dropped to the curve of her hips and something inside him stirred to life.

Kyle wanted her.

Around them, the clink of glasses and the conversations of the other guests became white noise, as if they were the only two in the room.

"I think you should have saved this for the runway," he whispered in her ear.

"Our collection makes this dress look like last season," she said.

"I doubt that. You look stunning, Zoe."

"Thank you for the compliment."

She stopped a passing waiter and ordered a white-chocolate martini. Then she turned to Kyle, who ordered a glass of white wine.

"Kyle, over here," a photographer said to them. Kyle wrapped his arm around Zoe as they posed for a picture.

"Excuse me." A young woman approached them. "I'm with *Fashion Forward* magazine. Fashion shows seem geared toward entertainment, and often what we see on the runway can't be found in stores. Would you care to comment?"

"A fashion show should be flashy and exciting. The shows are more about the designer's image than what ends up in stores," Zoe explained.

"That's what makes it a show, an event," Kyle interjected, smiling at Zoe.

As Kyle answered the reporter's questions, Zoe struggled to keep her attention on the interview. She fought the need for Kyle's touch, for the whisper of words she longed to hear him say—words that would never come out of his mouth.

Zoe hoped that her face did not betray her thoughts, particularly since there was a camera crew standing right there. When the reporter moved on to talk to someone else, she took a deep breath and turned to Kyle.

"I really didn't expect you to come to the party," she told him, ignoring the hum of tension simmering between them.

"You did invite me."

He smiled—the kind of smile that stirred the blood and brought desire bubbling to the surface. Not that Kyle needed a smile to ignite her desire. She could already think of nothing other than feeling his hands on her again.

"Yeah, but I didn't think you'd really come."

"I can't stay long, but I didn't want to disappoint you."

Before she could respond, they were joined by Jerry.

"I guess we should feel honored to have Kyle Hamilton grace us with his presence," Jerry said.

"Jerry—" Zoe began.

"It's fine," Kyle told her. "Your boss simply doesn't know any better. I'll go find us the drinks."

He strode away, leaving Jerry fuming.

"Why did you do that?" Zoe questioned.

"He is always so smug."

"I can't believe you sometimes, Jerry." She was just about to tell him that Kyle was at the party in good faith when Roberta Dallard made her entrance.

Zoe stole a glance at Kyle. He didn't seem to notice her arrival, as he was engaged in conversation with a department-store buyer.

Roberta, however, spotted him and quickly made her way over to where he was standing.

He appeared mildly surprised to see her.

But Zoe was even more surprised when Kyle abruptly left Roberta standing alone, watching him closely as he walked in her direction.

"You don't have to spend the evening with me," Zoe told him.

"The only reason I'm here is you."

She glanced over at Roberta and said, "Someone looks upset."

"I can't do anything about that," he said with a shrug, checking his watch. "I have to leave, but I hope we can get together soon. We still need to have that talk, Zoe."

"I know," she said. "It'll have to be when the time is right."

"I'll see you at RHD's party, right?"

Zoe nodded. "I'll be there."

"We'll find some time to talk then," he told her.

"But—"

Kyle placed a finger on her lips. "I won't take no for an answer."

She resisted the urge to watch him leave.

"This is a great party," Liora said when she walked up to Zoe. "I've gained a good five pounds already."

"That just means more time in the gym," Zoe said with a grin. "I'll be right there beside you. I've been munching all evening."

"It seems to me that a certain bachelor couldn't keep his eyes off you, Zoe."

"I don't know about all that," she said.

"I do," Liora teased with a smile.

"I see a few buyers I haven't greeted yet. Enjoy the rest of the party," Zoe said, trying to avoid talking to Liora about Kyle.

Liora let her off the hook. "A couple of friends

of mine and I are going to the Bianchi party. I'll probably be leaving in about ten minutes or so."

"Grab a goody bag for me," Zoe said. "Last year they gave out charm bracelets designed just for the event."

Alone, she chewed her bottom lip as she wondered what she would say to Kyle. Could she speak from her heart? Zoe wasn't sure.

"Can you believe that?" Sasha uttered in disgust to her coworker as she watched her nemesis floating around the room as if she were a VIP. They were seated at a table six rows from the front, which galled her to no end. "The media's treating Zoe like she's a star. Why should anybody care about her? She certainly didn't do any of this by herself."

"She's been getting a lot of attention from Kyle Hamilton," her coworker said.

Sasha followed the woman's gaze, and then saw Roberta Dallard standing nearby. "Looks like Roberta isn't too happy about that. I don't blame her at all. I wouldn't want my man anywhere near Zoe. She is definitely not to be trusted."

"Roberta looks like she's about ready to jump all over Zoe."

Sasha broke into a grin. "Now, that would be real entertainment."

"What are you two talking about?" Jerry asked, taking a seat beside Sasha.

Sasha wondered just how much of the conversation he had overheard. "Just some girl talk."

"I think I chose the wrong moment to come sit down. Maybe I should leave."

Sasha laughed. "Jerry, don't you dare. I haven't seen you all night."

"I've been running around catering to our VIPs. Now that Kyle's gone, Zoe can focus on work."

Sasha nodded as her eyes scanned the room. "Where's Roberta? Did she leave?"

Jerry glanced around. "I hope not. She wanted to talk to me about our show. Maybe she just went to the ladies' room."

"I don't know," Sasha murmured. "She looked pretty upset over something."

"Well, hopefully she's still here," he said. "But if not, I'll just give her a call in the morning."

Sasha exchanged a knowing glance with her co-worker. She knew that Zoe had feelings for Kyle and she wanted to see her with a broken heart. Someone needed to take Zoe down a peg or two.

"Kyle, what's going on between you and Zoe?"

Kyle turned around to face Roberta, a gathering tension spreading across his shoulders. "I'm sorry, but I'm in a hurry. Why don't I give you a call sometime tomorrow?"

He couldn't believe that she'd been standing outside the men's room waiting on him.

Kyle hoped that she wouldn't make a scene. He could feel the burn of eyes on them, could sense the attention their exchange had garnered in the hallway. He hoped they could keep this a civil conversation.

"I deserve an answer." Her voice took on a sharper edge than he'd ever heard from her. "I was under the impression that you and I were trying to—"

Kyle cut her off. "Roberta, I'm sorry if I gave you the wrong impression. I like you and I enjoy our friendship." He met her eyes, sincere in his words.

"Are you seeing Zoe?" The emotion in her voice spilled over into her eyes.

"No, I'm not."

"But you want to." The words snapped past her lips as a biting accusation. "You are attracted to her. I can see it whenever you look at her."

He did not respond. Roberta gave a sad shake of her head. "I'm disappointed in you, Kyle. You just don't know a good thing when you see it."

"Did it ever occur to you that maybe I don't deserve a woman like you?" Kyle didn't want to say anything to offend Roberta. After all, they had to work together and he didn't want to ruin that relationship.

She smiled. "Of course. I thought I'd give you a chance anyway."

"I hope that we can still be friends, Roberta."

She folded her arms across her chest. "I'll have to think about it."

He watched her as she sashayed back into the ballroom, relieved to have extricated himself from a complicated situation, and then headed toward a waiting elevator.

He called his mother as soon as he stepped into the elevator. "I'm on my way up," he told her.

Nelson rushed in behind him. "Hey, I thought you were gone already."

"I saw you talking to one of the Guava models and I figured you'd want to hang around for a while."

"Naw...all she wanted to talk about was herself."

Kyle laughed.

"How did things go between you and Zoe?" Nelson inquired.

He shrugged. "I'm not really sure. I've been honest with Zoe, but she doesn't seem to believe me." Kyle released a short sigh. "The thing is that I really care about her."

"I knew you did."

Kyle smiled. "I didn't realize just how much until recently. Only, now Zoe isn't giving me the time of day. I can't even get her to talk about it."

"Maybe she just needs some space. There's a lot going on this week."

"I know this week is crazy," he said. "But I don't want to put this discussion off."

"Is Zoe still coming to the party?" Nelson asked as they walked off the elevator.

"I think so," Kyle replied. "I hope she does. I just wish I hadn't told her to bring Jerry."

"He's quite the character," Nelson said. "My mother says that he is not to be trusted."

Kyle laughed. "He's a lot of talk, but when it comes down to it, he's harmless."

Kyle found his parents standing inside the Georgian Ballroom near the dance floor. They appeared to be deep in conversation with Cameron.

Kyle glanced at the tables set up with tropical floral centerpieces, the faux palm trees scattered around the room and the large aquarium of tropical fish that doubled as a podium. Another great RHD party, he thought. Just as he was about to greet his parents, he sensed Zoe's presence behind him. He turned around in time to see her walk through the doors with Jerry.

Once again he regretted his decision to invite her boss.

Kyle walked over to them. "Welcome to our tropical paradise."

"It's lovely in here," Zoe murmured. "I feel like I've been transported to the Caribbean."

Jerry looked as though he'd sucked on something sour.

"Would either of you like something to drink?"

"Why don't I get it?" Zoe said, obviously trying to give Kyle and Jerry a moment to talk.

Zoe politely excused herself, and Jerry turned to Kyle.

"You and Zoe seem to have gotten pretty close," Jerry stated. "I have to ask, is there something going on between you and my lead designer?"

"Maybe you should ask Zoe," Kyle said smoothly. "Not that it is any of your business."

"I won't let you hurt her."

"Jerry, are you concerned about Zoe, or concerned about *losing* Zoe?"

"I'm not at all worried. RHD had its chance. Zoe has no interest in leaving Guava."

Kyle smiled. "Perhaps if you keep telling yourself that, you will eventually believe it."

In a low voice, Jerry muttered, "I'm not going to sit around and let you steal her from my company."

"You mean the way you stole her from me?"

"Hey, don't get mad at me for your own mistakes, Kyle. Zoe didn't need a whole lot of convincing to jump ship and come to Guava. In fact, I got the impression that she couldn't sign on fast enough." Jerry gave him a sidelong glance. "What did you do to her?"

"Inviting you here was a mistake, but the damage has already been done. Nevertheless, I'm warning you, Jerry. Stay as far away from me as possible."

As Jerry stalked away, his words rang in Kyle's head. *What did you do to her?*

Kyle hated that he had done anything to Zoe to hurt her, to drive her away from RHD. He'd find a way to make it up to her. But first, they had to talk.

Kyle's gaze traveled the room, searching for one woman in particular.

He found her sitting with his mother at a table. His lips turned upward as he watched them talking and laughing.

She glanced up and met his gaze, granting him a tiny smile that he felt clear into his soul before she looked away.

It was time. He needed to get her alone and have that conversation before he lost any more of himself to beautiful Zoe Sinclair.

Zoe eased up beside her boss, taking him by the arm. "There are a couple of photographers heading in this direction, Jerry. You look like you've eaten sour candy, so you might want to change your facial expression."

"I actually tried making peace with Kyle, but it's not going to work, Zoe. I can't stand the man."

"I'm sure he feels the same way about you," Zoe said drily.

"I'm just saying—"

"I know what you're trying to say," she interjected. "Look, I came to the RHD party to network and have a good time. I suggest you do the same."

"Sometimes I think you forget who the supervisor in this relationship is," he said.

"Jerry, I am well aware that you're my boss, but the way you let Kyle get under your skin really frustrates me. He is not the enemy," she said.

He quickly pasted on a smile and posed with Zoe when a photographer stopped a few feet in front of them.

When the man walked away to snap pictures of one of the models, he turned to her and said, "Are you so sure about that, Zoe? I think he's trying to get you to go back to RHD."

"Oh, stop it, Jerry." She glanced toward the entrance and said, "Carmen Perez with *Women's Wear Daily* just arrived. Let's go say hello."

As Jerry let her lead him over to the editor, Zoe's mind was spinning. Was that what was going on with Kyle? Was this whole attraction thing a ruse just to lure her away from Guava?

Suddenly Zoe didn't know what to believe.

Chapter 10

"I want you to know that I'm really glad you came to RHD's party," Kyle said when he finally found Zoe standing near the entrance to the ballroom. "Are you ready for that chat now?"

"I should go over and say hello to the rest of your family while they are alone," Zoe told him. "I haven't spoken to your sisters yet."

Kyle nodded, aware that Zoe was avoiding their conversation.

"I'll walk you over," Kyle said as he took her arm to turn her around. Just the feel of her skin sent his pulse racing. He had to get her alone, and soon.

Zoe and Bailey embraced when they reached his family's table.

"It's so good to see you," Bailey said. "We never did have our girls' night out."

"Let's get through Fashion Week and then we can schedule some girl time."

"You promise?" Bailey questioned.

Zoe nodded as Nelson arrived.

"Hello, Nelson," she greeted. "How was your audition?"

"I think it went well, but we'll see." He looked her up and down. "I have to say that I don't know why you're not gracing the runway."

She laughed. "I've never had any desire to be a model. I've always wanted to be a designer. I've been designing clothes since I was old enough to sew."

"Kyle, do you mind if I dance with this beautiful woman?"

"I think you should ask Zoe," Kyle said with a chuckle. "This woman has her own mind."

"I would love to dance with you, Nelson."

As Kyle watched them on the dance floor, he realized that he was glad to see her enjoying herself. All he wanted was for her to be happy.

Because if Zoe was happy, maybe that would help tear down the wall she had built up around her heart.

And maybe then she'd let him in.

"I hope you didn't ask me to dance so that you could plead your cousin's case."

Nelson laughed. "No, I've decided it's far safer for me to just watch from the sidelines, but for the record—my money's on you, little lady."

She broke into a smile. "I knew from the moment we met that I'd like you."

"Same here." Nelson paused before saying, "I want you to know that Kyle is a good guy, Zoe."

"I thought you weren't going to plead his case."

"I'm not. I'm just stating the obvious."

She moved her body to the rhythm of the music as she thought about what Nelson had said. Was Kyle truly a good guy at heart? She found she wanted to believe that more than anything.

"You two looked pretty cozy out there," Kyle said after Nelson escorted her back to him.

She grinned. "You're not jealous, are you?"

"Would you like to take a walk with me?" he asked.

"Sure."

"I've been trying to get you alone for the past half hour," Kyle confessed when they stepped out onto the rooftop garden.

Zoe looked up, meeting his gaze. "Why have you been trying to get me alone? Do you have something pressing to discuss?"

He gave a short chuckle. "Why are we doing this?"

She gave him an innocent look. "Doing what?"

"Playing this game. Zoe, I can't stop thinking

about you. There's something between us and I know that you feel it, too."

"I won't deny that we're attracted to each other, but it doesn't mean that we should give in to that attraction."

"It's much more than attraction, and you know it."

"Actually, I don't," she countered. "What I do know is that you are not the type of man who wants to settle down or be tied to one woman. It's just not your style."

"A man can change."

"This is true, but it doesn't mean that you have, Kyle."

"Excuse me?"

"All I'm saying is that you may feel a certain way for the moment, but in the long run…you might change your mind."

"Zoe, I'm not saying that we have to rush into anything."

"Let's just leave things the way they are," Zoe suggested. "We made love in the heat of the moment. It doesn't tie us to each other."

"We can't just dismiss what happened that day in the supply room," Kyle said. "Zoe, I want more than sex. I want to give us a chance. I know that you want that, too. I can see it in your eyes."

With that, Kyle pulled her into his arms, kissing her passionately.

Her body reacted instantly. Despite everything, Zoe felt the swell of desire rising inside.

"What would a man have to do to change your mind?" he asked, his voice low and sensual.

For a charged moment, Zoe couldn't breathe as she stared into his dark and seductive eyes.

"I don't know," she whispered. Her gaze shifted to his mouth and Zoe knew she was doomed. She forced her attention away from his lips.

"Why do you keep fighting the inevitable?"

Zoe swallowed hard. "I'm simply using my head, Kyle. I refuse to be led by my heart." She bit her bottom lip when she realized that she'd said too much.

Kyle suddenly scooped her up in his arms and kissed her passionately again. It took every ounce of strength Zoe had to pull away from him. "I'm sorry."

"You don't have anything to apologize for," he assured her. "Don't be afraid of what we feel for each other."

"How am I supposed to risk everything on someone who has made it clear that he intends to be a bachelor for life?"

"Do you really believe that?" he asked. "Please give us the chance we deserve, Zoe."

He kissed her again. Her breathing was becoming ragged as her blood pumped through her veins like liquid fire. His kisses were electric, and her body still hungered to connect with his, but she was determined not to have a repeat of what had happened in the supply room, and some dark corner of her mind urged caution. A kiss was one thing, but Zoe was not ready for anything else. She needed to keep her desire for Kyle under control.

"What's wrong, sweetheart?"

"We can't do this, Kyle," she whispered. "I can't do this."

"Zoe—"

"No. What happened between us was a mistake. I'm not going to let it happen again."

"Why do you keep saying that it was a mistake?"

"Kyle, I know you. We don't want the same things when it comes to a relationship. I'm just not willing to compromise."

She wished it were different. Zoe wished that he could love her as she did him, but Kyle Hamilton wasn't the kind of man to commit. "I think it's best if we just put what happened behind us," she suggested. "You were right the first time. We should keep our relationship purely professional."

She did not bother to wait for a response. Zoe turned and started back inside the building.

She was not going to let Kyle break her heart all over again.

"Zoe, why are you making things so complicated?" Kyle demanded when he caught up with her.

"I'm not," she said. "I just think that we both need to focus on work right now. The shows start tomorrow, or have you forgotten?"

"This isn't over, Zoe. We have a lot to discuss. Will you at least meet me for dinner tomorrow night?" Kyle inquired.

"There's nothing to discuss."

He moved closer to her. "You say there's nothing going on…but why is it that right now all I can think about is kissing you, and doing my best to keep things at only a kiss, even though I want far, far more?"

She narrowed her eyes. "I'm not looking to be friends with benefits, Kyle."

"I care about you more than that, Zoe."

"You don't have to pretend something you don't feel."

His laugh sounded ragged, even to him. "Here's a little tip about me. There are certain things I just can't fake."

Her cell phone rang. She pulled it out of her purse and said, "It's Jerry."

Kyle shook his head.

"I'm sorry," Zoe murmured. "I need to see what he wants."

"Duty calls," he said. "But I want a rain check.

Can we at least meet for dinner tomorrow evening? I'll give you a call after the show."

She smiled after a moment. "I would love to have dinner with you."

"Great." Kyle let out a sigh of relief. "I've never had such a hard time asking a woman out."

"I'm not just any woman."

"You're right about that, Zoe."

Her phone rang again. Without looking at it, she said, "I really need to see what Jerry wants."

"I guess we need to get back downstairs, then," Kyle said.

When they reached the ballroom, Jerry was waiting for Zoe. He sent a sharp glance in Kyle's direction.

"What did you need?" she asked Jerry.

"I was wondering if you were ready to leave." He glanced over at Kyle. "It's getting late."

"If you'd like to stay, I can take you home," Kyle told her.

Zoe watched as the warmth disappeared from Jerry's eyes. His voice was hard when he spoke. "She came with me."

Zoe took a tentative step back. "Oh no, you two are not going to do this. I am leaving and I'm taking a taxi." Turning to Kyle, Zoe said, "I had a nice time. Thanks for inviting me."

He smiled. "You're welcome." Kyle planted a quick kiss on her cheek. "I'll walk you out."

Jerry muttered a curse and walked away in a huff.

"I'm sorry about that," Kyle told her. "I don't know why he is so territorial."

"He doesn't like you," Zoe said.

To her surprise, he laughed. "That's his problem. I'm not going to make it mine."

"Neither am I."

Jerry was seething and probably would not speak to her in the office tomorrow. He was temperamental and moody, but he did not frighten or intimidate Zoe.

She could handle Jerry.

It was Kyle she was worried about.

Chapter 11

The next day marked the beginning of Fashion Week. While fashion followers, celebrities, designers and other industry professionals flocked to the various white tents lined up at Lincoln Center, everyone at Guava was busy preparing for the show that was scheduled for Friday afternoon.

Zoe observed the models as they worked with the choreographer.

"How is it looking?" Jerry whispered when he eased into the room.

"It's all coming together," she said in a low voice.

"Okay, let's take a ten-minute break," the choreographer announced.

While they were all straight-faced during the rehearsal, the models oozed personality as they chatted on cell phones or listened to music on their break.

"Come outside," Jerry said. "I need to talk to you."

She nodded and followed him out of the room. Zoe had not been expecting to have a conversation with Jerry, especially after last night. He had ignored her most of the morning, forcing her to wait until he was ready to discuss what had happened.

"I have to be honest with you, Zoe. I don't like what went down last night. We went to that party together and we should have left together."

"It was not a date, Jerry. It was a work function."

"I know that," he said drily. "But you could've put on a unified front for the sake of Guava."

"You overreacted and I didn't appreciate being placed in the middle."

"I might as well tell you that I'm not crazy about this alliance you have with Kyle. As I told you before, I don't trust him."

"I used to work with Kyle. We *do* have a professional relationship, so I'm not sure I understand what you expect from me. We don't discuss what goes on here at Guava or at RHD."

"I know you would never betray the company in that way."

"Then what is the problem?" Zoe wanted to know. She was not about to allow Jerry to tell her who she could or could not talk to, and she would not let him drag her into the middle of his feud with Kyle, either.

"I know that you have issues with Kyle that go way back, but they don't have anything to do with me," she said. "I'm not going to be a part of that."

"He's only trying to get you to come back to RHD. Just think about it—all of this time you've been working at Guava and now he's suddenly interested in you? It's because your stock has gone up in value, so to speak. The world knows who you are, and—"

Zoe interrupted him. "I don't want to hear this."

"Is this how you let your subordinates talk to you?"

Zoe turned to see Sasha standing a few feet away.

"Why don't you mind your own business?" Zoe said.

Sasha brushed by Zoe with a chuckle. She stood beside Jerry with her arms folded across her chest.

"We were having a *private* conversation," Zoe said. "Not that you would know what that means."

"Jerry, you seriously need to tame your little pet before she gets hurt."

"Back into your neutral corners," he demanded. "Sasha, I need to talk to Zoe. Why don't you order us something to eat from the restaurant across the street? I'm not in the mood for anything on the cafeteria menu today."

"Excuse me?"

"You heard me. I'll seek you out after I finish talking to Zoe."

She glowered at Zoe before turning to leave.

"There really isn't anything else to say, Jerry. My relationship with Kyle is my business."

"I just don't want to see you being used as a pawn."

Zoe looked up, meeting his gaze head-on. "I won't allow myself to be used in that way by *anybody.*"

"I guess you're right, then. There's nothing more to be said."

She watched him stalk down the hallway. Zoe could tell he was angry, but she did not care. She had to draw a line when it came to her personal life.

Zoe did not believe for a second that Kyle was trying to manipulate her into leaving Guava. He would not do something like that—she was sure of it.

Wasn't she?

When Kyle and his family arrived at Lincoln Center, an intern rushed up to him, asking, "Have you seen Bailey? I thought she would be here by now. They're doing a run-through for the show."

"I haven't seen her," he replied. "My sister likes to be alone right before a show."

"Just tell the producer that she will be along shortly," Lila interjected. "Bailey is very reliable."

"Yes, ma'am," the intern said before rushing off.

Kyle knew that his sister always had her fittings completed the day before a show and often did not attend the last-minute rehearsals because she preferred to prepare on her own. Bailey would go over any last-minute changes with the producer and choreographer if necessary.

With a kiss on his mother's cheek, he said farewell and went backstage.

Nelson was already here somewhere, having left shortly after eight this morning to meet with the producer and show coordinator. Kyle had yet to run into him, but he knew that his cousin was on top of things. Nelson was a wonderful assistant and he doubted that he would ever find anyone to take his place.

Thinking of irreplaceable people brought Zoe to mind. He understood some of what scared her about him. She was right. There was a time when Kyle wanted nothing more than to be single. Actually, he had felt that way not too long ago.

But then he had ended up locked in a room with Zoe. Everything had changed for him then.

He was not going to let her down.

Convincing Zoe of that was quite the challenge, but he had never been one to easily give up. The fact that she had feelings for him increased his odds, Kyle decided.

He intended to woo her until she saw that he was the man she needed him to be.

Bailey was going to be a hit at the RHD fashion show for sure. Zoe really wished she could be there for Kyle and his sister. She couldn't even sneak over to the RHD tent for a quick peek. Jerry had everyone scurrying about, finalizing details.

She found Jerry standing in the hallway near his office on his cell phone, talking in a low voice, but he ended the call abruptly when he spotted her. "What are you doing?" he demanded. "I thought I told you to have the models do one more run-through."

"Jerry, you need to calm down," she said. "We're ready for tomorrow. Everything is perfect."

He glanced over at the collection of clothing on a rack nearby. "I want our launch to be better than perfect, Zoe. We want the world talking about every single piece of this spring/summer collection."

"And they will be," she assured him.

He gave her a tiny smile. "This is what I really like about you. You are always so optimistic."

"Why does it seem as though I always find the two of you in a corner somewhere whispering?"

They both turned to find Sasha standing in the doorway.

"You know, people are starting to talk," she said as she approached them, her hands on her hips.

"The only person talking is you," Zoe said, waving her hand in dismissal.

Jerry choked off a chuckle as Sasha glared at him.

"I need to get back to my office," Zoe announced as she headed to the door. She paused long enough to say, "Sasha, why don't you find something productive to do? In case you haven't noticed, we are extremely busy around here."

"Who do you think you are?" she challenged. "You may think you run things around here, but you do not."

"And neither do you, Sasha." Zoe struggled to keep her frustration in check. "We all have a lot of work to do, so why don't we get back to it?"

"Zoe's right," Jerry said. "Back to work."

In the hallway, Sasha stood blocking Zoe's path with her arms folded across her chest. "I'm tired of you trying to boss me around."

"This isn't about you, Sasha."

"You may have Jerry fooled, but I know you."

"Move out of my way."

"I have worked hard to prove my loyalty to

Guava and to Jerry," Sasha said. "You, on the other hand, would go running back to RHD in a heartbeat."

Zoe chuckled as she stepped around Sasha. "That just proves that you don't know me at all."

"I'm sorry for interrupting, but where is Bailey?" Brianna asked Kyle. "She's needed in hair and makeup."

Kyle was backstage going over the seating chart with the RHD publicist. "I haven't seen her," he said. "But she'll show up in time."

Daniel agreed. "Bailey is probably off somewhere meditating."

The publicist excused herself by saying, "I'll be with your mother if you need me."

"Kyle, I've looked everywhere for her. She's usually not gone this long."

He glanced over at his sister. "Don't worry, Brianna. You know Bailey. She likes to go off alone to prepare for a show."

"It's just not like her to completely disappear like this."

"She's probably in makeup by now," Daniel said. "I bet you'll find her there."

She looked from one brother to the other. "So you don't think there's any reason to be worried?"

"I don't," they replied in unison.

"I'll go back to hair and makeup," Brianna said. "I have some words for our sister."

"Don't be too hard on her," Kyle said. "This is the first time she's ever been late to anything."

He strode past a refreshment table lined with yogurt, soda, muffins and plenty of coffee and tea. A group of robed models stood nearby talking and checking their phones while waiting for makeup stations to open up.

He removed a dress from the plastic bag and felt a surge of pride in his handiwork.

"It's a work of art."

Kyle turned to face his mother. "I appreciate the compliment. My inspiration came while I was in Jamaica watching the sunset. The designs are all hand painted."

"Fabulous," Lila murmured.

"So have you seen Zoe lately?" she asked.

Kyle broke into a grin. "Mom, are you still trying to find a wife for me?"

"I simply asked if you'd seen Zoe recently."

"As a matter of fact, I saw her at the RHD party. And so did you."

Lila gave him a slight pinch. "Smarty-pants."

He laughed. "I'm going to see her later tonight, Mom. We have a date."

"I'm so happy for you."

"I thought you would be," Kyle said.

"Zoe is a really sweet, talented girl and she seems perfect for you."

"I'm beginning to feel the same—"

Kyle never got to finish his thought.

Brianna rushed up to them. "Bailey is missing."

Lila gasped.

"She's not with the hairstylist?" Kyle asked.

"We've looked everywhere. Daddy is talking to the head of security now. The show begins in an hour. If we don't find her, what are we going to do?"

"We *are* going to find her," Kyle stated.

"I need to go to your father," Lila said.

"Take Mom to the security office," Kyle directed. "I'm going to grab Nelson and we're going to do a little search of our own."

A thread of fear snaked down Kyle's spine.

Nelson met him at the door of Bailey's dressing room. "Have you heard?"

He nodded. "Let's search through every room, including the closets. Zoe and I were locked in the supply room at the Childs Hotel. Maybe someone is playing a cruel joke."

"Well, it's not funny," Nelson said as he and Kyle headed down the hallway.

"I'll start down there and you start at the other end," he suggested.

Nelson gave a slight nod. "We're going to find her."

"Kyle, you go on and get dressed," his father called after him. "Security's looking all over for Bailey. If she's here, they'll find her. But we need to keep this under wraps for now."

"But Bailey—"

"Brianna's taking her place. She's with the hairstylist now."

"Dad, what's going on?"

Roger shook his head. "I don't know and I don't want to make any assumptions."

Kyle didn't want to assume anything, either. To do so would only make them more uneasy. He struggled to keep from fearing the worst.

"Go on, son," Roger prompted. "Get dressed."

Kyle's stomach knotted up and he suddenly felt sick. He blamed himself for not going to look for her when Brianna first came to him. This was his fault and if anything happened to Bailey, he would never forgive himself.

Please, Lord, let my sister be okay. Help us to find her, he prayed.

Zoe checked her watch. As expected, she'd heard nothing from Kyle. He was supposed to have called by now to discuss the details of their date, which was why she'd checked her cell phone three times in the past thirty minutes.

I was right, she thought. *He wants nothing more to do with me.*

Zoe was angry with herself for falling for his empty words. She vowed this would be the last time. He would not be able to hurt her like this ever again.

Her cell phone rang.

A wave of disappointment flowed through her when Liora's name, not Kyle's, came up.

"Hey, what's up?" Zoe asked.

"I was thinking about going to the Marc Jacobs party tonight. Do you want to come with?"

"No, I'm not really up for another party. I think I'll just come home and get into bed."

"Are you okay?" Liora inquired. "You sound a little down."

"I'm fine," Zoe answered, checking her watch yet again. "I'll give you a call later."

"Sure you don't want to hang out for a little while?"

"I don't feel up to it."

"Okay. Well, I might be gone by the time you get home. If I don't talk to you later, I'll see you in the morning."

"Have fun," Zoe told her roommate. She was relieved to have the apartment to herself because she was not in a great mood. In fact, she was furious with herself for believing any of the words that had ever come out of Kyle's mouth.

But at this point, she had no one to blame but herself.

Chapter 12

After the show, Kyle gathered everyone together.

"When did you last see my sister?" He and his parents were backstage with the models. "We need to know if anyone saw anything, whether you think it's important or not."

His inquiry was met with silence.

He shook his head in confusion. This was the biggest show of the season. Bailey wouldn't have missed it for anything. Something was very, very wrong.

Kyle glanced over at his mother. She looked worried sick and he couldn't blame her.

The head of security entered the room and was immediately met by Kyle's father.

"We're going to find Bailey," Kyle whispered as he wrapped an arm around his mother. "We *will* find her."

"Everybody is wondering what's going on," she whispered. "We don't want the media getting wind of Bailey's disappearance—not until it is absolutely necessary. We need to make sure everyone understands."

"Do you think she's been kidnapped?" Brianna asked in a low voice. Her eyes were bright with tears.

Kyle shook his head. "Let's not jump to conclusions."

"This isn't like Bailey," Lila said. "Something has happened to my daughter. I can feel it."

The security guards left as his father asked the staff and the models not to say anything publicly.

Kyle was worried about his mother. He had never seen her so scared, although she was trying hard to maintain her composure. He signaled to Nelson to escort her to a chair and get her a glass of water.

This was not the way the day was supposed to go. A wave of anger flashed through him. Had someone kidnapped his sister? His fingers clenched into a fist. If anyone laid a hand on Bailey…

He searched his mind, trying to think of anyone who would want to hurt his family.

"They've found her," Brianna announced, rushing toward Kyle.

"Where is she?" Kyle asked, hearing the desperation in his own voice.

"Kyle, Bailey was locked in a janitorial closet in Lincoln Center."

Before his sister could say another word, Kyle sprinted out of the tent and across the plaza with Nelson on his heels. By the time they got there, his father was sitting on the floor with an unconscious Bailey in his arms.

"An ambulance is on the way," he said.

Lila gasped when she saw her daughter. "Is she..."

"She's unconscious," Kyle said. "They have already called an ambulance."

"Who found her?" his mother asked.

"One of the janitors," Roger said.

"This was found with her," a security guard said, holding up a bag of cocaine.

"That doesn't belong to my sister," Kyle said. His tone brooked no argument. His sister was missing for hours and then found with cocaine—none of this was making sense.

"Does anybody know what happened?" Lila wanted to know. "What's wrong with her? Was she drugged?"

"We won't know until she gets to the hospital." Roger shook his head sadly. "Who could have done this to my daughter? If this gets out, it could ruin her."

Kyle watched as his mother gently stroked Bailey's hair. The look of fear on Lila's face crushed him. His hands clenched into fists. He wanted to kill the person responsible for doing this to his sister.

"I know what you're thinking, Kyle," Nelson said. "For now, just be grateful that she's okay."

"We don't know that for sure," he said.

"My mother wanted me to call her with any news." Nelson pulled out his cell phone. "She was really worried about Bailey."

Kyle walked over and placed an arm around his mother. "I told you that she would be found." He could not put into words the relief he felt at finding his sister.

The ambulance arrived.

Working quickly, they placed Bailey on a gurney and wheeled her out of the building.

Lila chose to ride in the ambulance to the hospital while the rest of the family rode with Kyle.

Zoe walked into a large conference room that had been taken over by hundreds of silver gift bags, which included an Aztec-print scarf from their new collection. She immediately began helping Jill, the administrative assistant at Guava.

"Zoe, I'm surprised you didn't attend the RHD

fashion show," Jill commented as she placed the giveaways into a box. "I heard that you're really close to the Hamiltons."

"Jill, do yourself a favor and stop listening to Sasha," Zoe said. "She really has no idea what she's talking about, especially when it comes to me or my relationships. Do you have all the accessories packed?"

Jill nodded. "I've gone over the checklist twice. I also went back over the shoes. Everything is packed and ready."

"Good," Zoe murmured.

"Are you okay?" Jill inquired. "You're not your usual smiling self."

"I'm fine." Zoe paused for a brief moment before saying, "I need to make sure everything is properly tagged."

"I did that already," Jill assured her. "Between you and Jerry, I don't know who's more nervous."

"I would say that it's Jerry," Zoe said. "But I admit that I'm feeling a tad anxious about tomorrow."

"Our collection is going to be the talk of Fashion Week, and so are your pieces."

Zoe gave Jill a tiny smile. "I think I'm going to call it a night. Tomorrow is going to be a long day."

"See you bright and early in the morning."

Zoe went back to her office and checked her voice mail.

She still had not heard from Kyle.

"I'm done," Zoe whispered as she grabbed her purse.

She caught sight of Sasha sauntering toward Jerry's office as she made her way to the elevator. Zoe shook her head. *That woman is nothing but trouble.*

She didn't want to think about Sasha, Jerry or Kyle. The only thing on her mind now was the pint of ice cream waiting for her back at the apartment.

A photograph of Bailey Hamilton appeared on the television in the break room as Zoe walked past. She paused in her steps to listen.

The reporter was discussing the model's unexplained disappearance at the RHD fashion show. Some speculated that she had gotten ill, but others suggested that she was missing.

Zoe gasped. A wave of shock coursed through her body. *Bailey's missing.*

Her disappointment in Kyle vanished at the news of Bailey's disappearance. She pulled out her cell phone.

"Kyle, I just heard the news," Zoe said as soon as he answered the phone. "Is there anything I can do for you? I was so scared when I heard about Bailey."

"I'm sorry for not calling you—"

"No, it's fine. I understand. I'm still in shock. Does anyone know—"

Kyle cut her off. "Bailey's been found. Zoe, I can't discuss this over the phone. Can you meet me at my place in about an hour?"

"Of course. I'll see you there."

Zoe felt guilty for thinking the worst of Kyle when in reality, his sister had gone missing.

She had never heard him sound so worried. At one point in the conversation, she was sure that he had been on the verge of tears. Her heart was breaking for him.

Bailey and Kyle were very close. He was close to his other siblings as well, but with her, they shared a special bond.

As soon as Zoe walked into Kyle's apartment, he pulled her into an embrace.

"Thank you for coming," he said, his voice ragged.

He led her through the living room to a den. If Bailey hadn't been at the forefront of her mind, Zoe would have delighted in Kyle's exquisite taste when it came to decorating.

"What happened?" she asked, taking a seat in one of the chairs near the fireplace. "Please tell me that Bailey's okay."

"She's as well as can be expected, I guess," he said. "I'm sorry I didn't call you earlier, but—"

"Kyle, you don't have to apologize. I understand," she said. "Where's Nelson?"

"He's with the rest of the family at my parents' apartment. I just needed…some time to myself."

"Was Bailey kidnapped?"

"All we know is that Bailey never made it to the fashion show, so Brianna ended up taking her place on the runway. While the show was going on, my dad had security looking all over Lincoln Center for her." His expression was full of pain. "Zoe, I've never been so scared in my life."

She reached over and took his hand. All she could think of was offering some small comfort. He had been through quite an ordeal.

"One of the security guards found my sister in a closet, unconscious. There was a bag of cocaine with her."

"There's no way it was hers. She doesn't take drugs," Zoe stated.

"I know that," Kyle said. "I'm sure the hospital tests will confirm that, as well."

"Unless someone forced her to take the cocaine," Zoe suggested, shocked at the very thought.

"Someone is out to hurt Bailey." Kyle's mouth tightened. "They could've killed my sister and we have no idea why."

"This is really crazy," she murmured. "Why would anyone want to hurt Bailey? She doesn't have any enemies."

"Apparently she does. I am going to find out

who did this, Zoe. When I do..." Kyle let the threat die on his lips.

"Where is Bailey now?"

"She's in the hospital. We have security outside her room. My parents are considering sending her away for a while. Her whereabouts will be kept secret. It's for her safety."

Zoe nodded in understanding. "I don't blame them."

"This was not what I had in mind when I said I wanted to see you tonight." He wrapped an arm around her. "But I'm glad you're here."

"I'll be here as long as you need me," Zoe said.

For so long, she'd thought of him only as a player, as a man only interested in getting as many women as possible into his bed. She'd thought he wasn't interested in anything but momentary pleasure.

Tonight, she'd seen glimpses of a different man.

He was watching her now.

"Why are you looking at me like that?" she asked softly. His gaze sent tiny sparks of desire through her body.

"You know, the first time I saw you I thought you had such a huge chip on your shoulder," Kyle told her.

"I didn't have a chip. I just couldn't stand you."

He quirked an eyebrow. "Really?"

Zoe nodded. "I thought you were a spoiled rich

kid who inherited his position, but once I began working with you, I knew I was wrong about you. I saw how hard you worked."

"My assumptions about you were wrong, too," Kyle said. "Tell me something. Why did you leave RHD?"

"I thought it was the best thing to do at the time," Zoe confessed. "I felt that you and I could not work together."

"Do you still feel that way?"

She nodded. "I always felt like we were in competition, and it's not supposed to be that way. At Guava, we really work as a team and I like that."

"I'm glad that you're happy there. Mostly I'm glad that they treat you well."

"They do," she confirmed.

A part of her expected some kind of cocky response. But instead, he said, "I hope that you get everything you want out of life, Zoe. You certainly deserve it."

"Where is all this coming from, Kyle?"

"I want you to trust me, and in order for that to happen, I have to be completely honest with you."

A smile played at the corner of her lips. "I appreciate that." She watched as a shadow of sadness darkened his gaze. "You're thinking about your sister, aren't you?"

Kyle nodded. "I have to go back to the hospital."

"I'd like to go with you, if you think it's okay."

"Bailey would love to see you."

She touched his cheek. "She's going to be fine. Your sister is a fighter and she will get through this."

"Thank you, Zoe. Thank you for being here for me. I can't tell you what it means to me."

Kyle gave Zoe a look of gratitude that she felt all the way to her soul, and she knew she was done for.

There was no escaping Kyle Hamilton now.

Chapter 13

Kyle and Zoe slipped into the private suite where Bailey was staying. The bodyguard standing outside the room had been instructed that no one was to enter her room outside of medical staff and family. They were not taking any chances and Zoe could not blame them. There were still no clues as to what had happened.

Bailey looked so pale lying in the private hospital bed. Her eyelids fluttered open when they neared.

Zoe was relieved to see that she only had some minor bruising around her mouth and on her arms, as if she'd been tied up. Zoe could barely suppress a shudder.

"I'm sorry. I didn't mean to wake you," Zoe whispered. "I just wanted to see for myself that you were okay."

"Zoe, I'm glad you came," she said softly. Bailey glanced over at Kyle and gave him a tiny smile.

"We're not going to stay too long," he told her. "We just came to check on you."

"I'm fine—just sleepy."

Kyle reached down and gave her hand a light squeeze. "Go back to sleep. I'll come back in the morning."

Bailey closed her eyes and was soon sound asleep.

Zoe and Kyle crept out of the room.

"Thank you for allowing me to see Bailey," Zoe told Kyle as they stepped into the elevator.

"I could see how worried you were and I know Guava's show is tomorrow. I didn't want there to be any distractions for you."

She smiled at him. "Thanks."

"I'll drop you off at home," he said. "As for our date, I really hope that you'll give me a rain check."

Zoe nodded. "Of course. When Fashion Week is over."

"This week has been interesting, to say the least."

"Yeah," she agreed. "I've heard other designers talk about mishaps before shows, but this is the first time I've experienced it. First we get locked in a room, and then someone kidnaps Bailey? It's strange, don't you think, Kyle?"

"I think that they must have panicked or something," Kyle said. "When they realized that they couldn't get her out of the building without being seen, they planted drugs on her to make it look like she did this to herself."

"Do you think she has a stalker?" It was a question that she knew was on Kyle's mind.

"I really don't want to consider the theory, but I don't know what else to think." Kyle shook his head. "That's why it's best that she go away for a while."

They grabbed a cab, and Kyle gave the driver Zoe's address.

"Give me a call if you need to talk, Kyle. We can talk all night."

"Your show is tomorrow. I won't keep you up all night."

Zoe was touched by his consideration. "That's sweet, but I mean it."

He shook his head. "No, I want you to focus on your show. Call me after everything's done if you feel up to it. I was planning to be there, but with everything that's going on, I'm just not sure. But, Zoe, I wish you the best of luck tomorrow."

"Thank you, Kyle."

When the cab pulled up at her building, Kyle

asked the driver to keep the meter running, got out and walked her up to the apartment.

"You didn't have to come up, but I do appreciate it," she told him.

"I'll rest better knowing that you are safe and sound in your place." Kyle pulled her into his embrace.

"Everything is going to be okay," she assured him, relishing the feel of his strong arms around her.

"I hope so."

Zoe was nearly overwhelmed by the urge to comfort Kyle, to pull him into her apartment and just hold him. But she knew that the smart thing to do, for both of them, was to say good-night.

Relief swept through Kyle when Bailey walked into the apartment with their parents the next day. He had never been so happy to see his sister in all his life. Her physical injuries were minimal, although she still appeared shaken by the terrifying experience.

She slowly sat down on the sofa.

Kyle sat down beside her. "I hated seeing you in that hospital bed."

"Trust me, I hated being there," she said. "I know you all want answers about what happened to me, but I really don't have any. I went to Lincoln Center early and went straight to the dressing room." Bailey paused a moment before continuing. "Someone grabbed me from behind and they put something over my nose and mouth. All I remember is that the smell reminded me of alcohol, and then everything grew dark."

"Unfortunately, it's being reported that you were was high on drugs, Bailey," Nelson said. "Someone snapped a picture of you and sold it."

Kyle muttered a curse under his breath.

"Honey, your father and I think that you should leave the country for a while," Lila said. "You can recuperate away from the glare of the media."

"She shouldn't be alone," Kyle said. "We need to make sure she is surrounded by security until we find out who's after her."

"I've hired bodyguards to travel with Bailey," Roger announced. "They'll leave tonight for an undisclosed location. She doesn't need to deal with public opinion after all she's been through."

Kyle agreed with his father. But he was also worried that whoever had attacked Bailey was still out there and would try again.

"I'm going to find out who leaked that photograph," he vowed. "Maybe that will lead us to the attacker."

"I read that Bailey had cocaine on her when she was found," Liora said as she poured herself a cup of coffee. "It was in one of the tabloids at the grocery store."

"It's not true," Zoe said. "I've known her for years and Bailey has never done drugs. She doesn't even like to take aspirin for a headache. She's being set up."

"Have you spoken to Kyle at all this morning?"

Zoe shook her head. "I left early to make sure that everything was ready at Lincoln Center. I only came back here because in my haste, I left this." She held up her iPad.

Liora chuckled. "I was wondering why you were here when I got up."

Picking up her purse, she said, "I need to head back, so I'll see you at the show."

"I'm looking forward to it."

A bouquet of roses had arrived for Zoe at the Guava tent while she was gone. She removed the tiny envelope attached.

> I wanted to wish you good luck with your show today.
> Kyle

"Who sent you those?" Jerry asked. "And where have you been? I've been looking everywhere for you."

"They're from Kyle," Zoe said. "As for where

I've been, Jerry, I was here at five-thirty this morning making sure that everything was in place." She swallowed the resentment she felt. He had been riding her all morning. Actually, he'd been riding her since the night of the cocktail parties.

"I'm sorry for growling at you," he said. "It's just that today of all days..."

"I told you that I would never let you down. And I haven't, Jerry." Zoe brushed past him without waiting for a response.

"I see one of the skeletons fell out of your precious Hamiltons' closet," Sasha said as Zoe walked past her. "I never would've imagined Bailey as a cokehead."

Zoe resisted the urge to strangle the woman.

She brushed past a group of models standing in line for hair and makeup. She set her roses on a table across from the refreshments.

Zoe released a soft sigh when she spotted Jerry walking toward her.

"We have a model that's running late. Her last show ran over," he complained. "I hate when this happens."

"Calm down," she told him. "They can do her makeup quickly and then she'll be ready. She's only a couple of tents away."

I'm not going to let anyone ruin this day for me, Zoe vowed silently when he walked away.

Her thoughts strayed more than once to Kyle, but she fought to bring her focus back to the show.

An hour later, she stood backstage next to Jerry as the show finally began. "We were only a few minutes late," Jerry said to Zoe. "That's not too bad."

"I told you to stop worrying so much," she said.

The third model was about to walk the runway wearing one of Zoe's designs. Zoe chewed on her bottom lip and resisted the urge to peek out at the attendees.

"Go, go," she heard the producer say. "C'mon, let's get out there."

After the finale, Jerry and Zoe walked out, hand in hand.

The room erupted in applause.

Smiling, Zoe waved at the buyers, fashion editors and others in attendance. She was proud of the fruits of her hard labor.

"What did I tell you?" Jerry said. "They loved your designs."

She smiled. "They loved yours, too. *We* were a hit." Zoe was ecstatic. The only low point was the fact that Kyle had not been able to share this moment with her.

"We should celebrate tonight," Jerry said. "Why don't we go to the Paradise Club?"

"Sounds like a plan," Sasha said. "Count me in."

He looked at Zoe. "You're going to join us, aren't you?"

Her eyes strayed to Sasha, who clearly didn't want Zoe to attend. Sasha didn't have to worry about her, however. Zoe wanted nothing more than to check on Kyle.

"I'm not going to be able to make it," she told him. "You all go and have a great time."

Sasha broke into a smile. "We intend to do just that. Don't we, Jerry?"

"Are you sure you don't want to come?" Jerry asked her, looking at her closely.

"I have other plans, I'm afraid." She pointed toward the rack of discarded clothing. "I'll start packing up."

"I'm going out to speak with a couple of editors," Jerry said. "I promised them interviews."

Zoe's cell phone rang as she was doing a quick inventory to make sure every outfit, pair of shoes and accessory was accounted for.

Her heart skipped a beat when she saw it was Kyle.

"Kyle, how is Bailey?" she asked as soon as she answered.

"She's coping with everything," he said. "She's talking to the police right now, but she doesn't really remember much of what happened."

"How are you?"

"I'm fine."

"No, you're not," she told him. "I can tell by your voice."

"I'm upset that somebody sold a photograph of my sister unconscious with a bag of coke. She is not a drug addict and I will not see her defamed."

"Kyle, anybody that knows your sister will know that it's not true."

"What about the millions who don't know her, Zoe?"

"The truth will come out."

There was a long pause. Zoe could tell Kyle wanted to ask her something. She held her breath.

"Zoe, would you like to spend the evening with me? We can order in and watch a movie or just talk."

Zoe couldn't help the giant grin that spread across her face. "I'd love that, Kyle. I'll be there as soon as I can." Zoe saw Jerry coming toward her and said, "I have to get back to work, but I'll see you later."

"Sounds like you have a big date tonight," Jerry said, sounding annoyed.

She smiled. "I wouldn't exactly call it a date, but I do have plans with a friend."

"Anybody I know?"

Zoe gave him a firm look that clearly said it was not any of his business. She knew that Jerry meant well, but there was a boundary he would not be allowed to cross.

* * *

"I have a good idea who she's spending the evening with," Sasha told Jerry.

"How would you know anything about Zoe's personal life? She can't stand you."

"Jerry, I'm going to give you a little piece of advice. You need to be very careful who you allow in your inner circle. There are some people who will do whatever it takes to make it in this industry, including betraying those she works with." Sasha took a sip of her champagne as she watched him over the rim of her glass.

"So? Who do you think Zoe is seeing tonight?"

She met Jerry's curious gaze. "I think you can answer that question yourself."

"Kyle Hamilton."

Sasha nodded. "She's involved with him."

Jerry shook his head. "He's just using her."

"I wish he would just take her back at RHD. We'll be fine without her."

"No," Jerry said. "I am not going to let Kyle win. Not this round."

"What do you plan to do?" Sasha asked with a look of delighted surprise.

"I'm not sure yet," Jerry said. "But Zoe is Guava's rising star, and she's not going anywhere. Not if I have anything to say about it."

Chapter 14

"Your show was a hit," Kyle said when she arrived at his apartment. "You're blowing up all over social media. Congratulations."

Zoe broke into a smile. "Thanks. I read in the *Times* this morning that RHD hit a home run as well, but then, I'm not surprised."

He eyed her for a moment. "You really seem to be in your element with Guava."

"I love what I do," she said. "I believe that designing is in my blood."

"It's true. You're very talented, Zoe."

She followed him through the apartment to the den, where the television was on.

"How is Bailey doing?" Zoe inquired.

"She's okay for the most part. I know that she's not sleeping well. She's still staying with my parents for now."

"So what are you working on now?" she asked, dropping down on the leather couch. "Have you already moved on to the collection for the fall?"

"Not yet. I've been playing with several ideas, but nothing's concrete."

His response stunned Zoe. He was not one to sit around idly. Kyle was usually way ahead of the game. In the past, he'd had the next collection sketched out by the end of Fashion Week.

"Kyle, are you okay?" she asked.

"Yeah," he said. "I just wish that I knew who was after my sister."

She reached over and squeezed his arm. "At least she's safe now."

"We just have to keep her that way." Kyle took her hand for a moment and gave it a squeeze. "Let's eat. I ordered us Italian."

As they sat at the dining room table, Kyle gazed at her. "I'm glad you came over, Zoe," he told her.

"So am I," she said. Zoe picked up her wineglass and took a sip. "After the day I've had, this is a nice way to relax."

Kyle broke into a grin. "I understand. So are you ready to see what your fans are saying about you?" Kyle handed her his phone, and she looked at the Guava Facebook feed.

Zoe smiled as she read what some of the attendees were saying.

> The first highlight came the moment Harley Paul stepped onto the catwalk in a stunning black shantung silk-and-lace gala creation by Zoe Sinclair. Last season she dazzled, but this year she outdid herself with a dramatic collection.

"It's a good feeling, isn't it?" Kyle asked her.

Zoe nodded.

"Just from the pictures I've seen so far, you and Jerry outdid yourselves. I won't be surprised if Jerry gets his own label soon."

"He's earned it," she said.

"Zoe, I'm really proud of you. I want you to know that."

She broke into a wide grin. "It means a lot to me to hear you say that."

Zoe and Kyle returned to the den after they finished eating.

"Still in the mood for that movie?" he asked.

"Actually," she confessed, "I'm tired."

"I'll give you a ride home."

"You don't have to do that."

"No, I want to," Kyle insisted. "I'm going to take you home."

She smiled. "Thanks, I appreciate it."

Zoe was touched that he was not going to try to get her to spend the night at his apartment. She knew that if he really pressed the issue it would not be easy for her to turn him down. Her body craved his touch, although she was working feverishly to keep the craving under control.

She didn't know how much longer she could keep up her guard. And she was starting to wonder why she bothered in the first place.

There was nothing more dangerous than that.

The next morning, Jerry stopped her in the hallway. "How was your date last night?"

"It was fine," she said, meeting his gaze. "How was your little party?"

"Oh, we had a good time." He followed her into her office. "I'm sure you've heard about Bailey Hamilton."

Zoe nodded. "Yes, I've heard the lies that the media is spreading."

"Lies? I know that you have a fondness for the Hamilton family, but pictures don't lie, Zoe. She was found with a bag of coke and she was clearly so high that she couldn't model. Her sister had to take her place."

"Bailey is not abusing drugs."

Jerry waved his hand as if to dismiss her words. "People have been known to live secret lives, Zoe."

"Bailey would never use cocaine."

"I wasn't aware that you and she were so close."

She met his gaze head-on. "That's because my relationship with Bailey has nothing to do with this job."

Jerry cleared his throat. "Well, I'm glad she's okay. I'm sure the Hamiltons were worried."

"We all were," Zoe murmured.

"Kyle is lucky to have you to comfort him."

"If you're going to get started on your rant about Kyle, I would rather not listen to it. I have work to do."

She was not in the mood for Jerry's attacks on Kyle. She knew that he was fishing around to find out the extent of their relationship, but Jerry had no right to delve into her personal life. He was her boss, but Zoe intended to make sure he did not cross any boundaries with her. It was a lesson she had learned from Kyle.

With Fashion Week behind them, Kyle and his family worked nonstop with police and private detectives, all looking for some clue as to who might be stalking Bailey. The Hamiltons also had to deal with the ever-intrusive press, who wanted to find more evidence of Bailey's drug use.

"They just won't let up," Kyle complained to Zoe one afternoon while they were having lunch.

"Even after releasing the toxicology results, people are still trying to prove that Bailey was high the day of the fashion show."

"Have the detectives come up with anything?"

He shook his head. "They have interviewed everyone Bailey may have encountered that day, but they've come up with nothing."

While Kyle knew that Zoe sincerely cared for Bailey, he wanted to keep his emotions intact. Just a few weeks ago, she would barely say two words to him.

"Hey," she prompted. "What are you thinking about?"

"It's nothing," Kyle replied.

"Are you sure?"

He nodded.

Zoe didn't press him any further.

Kyle cautioned himself to slow down where she was concerned. He had shown her what kind of man he was. Tried to make sure Zoe understood that she had someone to count on. She could let down all her defenses with him.

Only she chose to continue keeping her feelings locked up. Zoe had been so upset with him all these years—Kyle was not sure that she could just let the past die down completely. Was it possible that she was out for some type of revenge?

Zoe was not the type of woman who would

play games. But then again, she could hold on to a grudge. Kyle knew that much. She had also flirted with his cousin to make him jealous. He shook the troubling thoughts away. He was running out of reasons to keep his distance from Zoe. She was in his blood and there would be no escape.

Zoe left Kyle's apartment puzzled by his behavior. She knew that he was upset by the media's portrayal of Bailey and worried for her, but there seemed to be something else bothering him. She could see it in the lines of his face. Hear it in the strain of his voice.

She could feel it in the pit of her stomach.

He was distant in much the same way he had been all those years ago. When she'd readied herself to leave, Zoe had had the distinct impression that Kyle was relieved, and it brought back all the pain she had struggled to keep buried.

What kind of cruel game was Kyle playing? Did he have any idea how much she wanted him in her life, how afraid she was to let him near her heart? She didn't want him to shatter her world like he had five years ago.

Kyle had been pursuing her zealously, but since Bailey's kidnapping he suddenly seemed to be backing off. Maybe all he wanted from her was friendship.

But was that possible, after the kiss he had given her that night?

Zoe decided it was best to just keep her heart shielded. She had no interest in getting sucked back into the vortex of churning emotions—shame, embarrassment, anger and frustration. She wasn't going there again.

"You don't deserve my love, Kyle Hamilton," she whispered. The words opened an emptiness inside her.

Zoe made a cup of hot tea and carried it to her bedroom. She climbed into her bed and just sat there staring into space. A lone tear rolled down her cheek.

The words, the laughter, the intensity of the connection between them…was it simply Kyle reeling her in? Was he securing her attraction so that she would become his lover? His friend with benefits?

A part of her did not want to believe this of him. Would he be this cruel to intentionally hurt her?

No, Zoe thought. A connection like the one between them couldn't be faked.

Could it?

There was another option. It was possible Kyle had been as deeply affected by their connection as she had and found that it was too much for him to handle.

Maybe all he needed was time.

Maybe she was just a fool.

Zoe broke down into sobs at the revelation that Kyle did not love her, no matter how strong their connection, and that was the raw truth of it.

This was supposed to be one of the happiest times of her life.

She should have known better than to let Kyle back into her life.

Lesson learned.

"How are things between you and Zoe?" Nelson inquired.

"Okay, I guess."

"Just okay?"

Kyle met his cousin's gaze. "I care for her more than I could ever have imagined. I'm just not sure Zoe feels the same way."

"I can't believe you would doubt Zoe's feelings for you," Nelson said as he and Kyle were having breakfast in the cafeteria at RHD. "Has Zoe ever given you any reason to doubt her?"

"No, not really," he said. "How is a relationship between us going to work?"

"You two can make this work, Kyle. Especially if it's what you both want."

He shrugged. "I don't know. Right now my mind is messed up. This thing with Bailey really bothers me."

"Your sister is safe in an unknown location and no one can get to her."

Kyle picked up the newspaper and sighed. "Yet another article about Bailey." He read it from beginning to end before saying, "There's a quote in here from Zoe."

Nelson wiped his mouth on his napkin. "What does it say?"

"She's defending Bailey."

"You can't be surprised, Kyle."

"No, I'm not. I know she really cares about my sister."

"She also cares about you," Nelson said. "If you don't wise up, you may end up losing Zoe for good."

Kyle considered Nelson's words. A thread of guilt snaked down his spine.

He reached for the phone and dialed.

The drumbeat of rain on the balcony that had lasted most of the afternoon gradually faded to silence as Zoe worked on a new design in her office. Her stomach growled. She was so immersed in her work that she hadn't bothered to eat lunch.

Her door was closed, a signal to her coworkers that Zoe did not want to be disturbed. Not even Jerry ventured inside unless it was an urgent matter. She appreciated that he respected her space when she was in creative mode.

Zoe picked up a couple of fabrics and held them out toward the light.

Her lips formed a smile as her eyes traveled back to the vivid purple silk in her left hand. She laid it next to a mint-green sample in ponte knit.

Zoe tacked the fabrics on her sketch.

The ringing of her cell phone pulled her away from her drawing.

When she saw Kyle's name on the caller ID, Zoe paused. Then she answered. "Hello, Mr. Hamilton. How are you?"

He paused for a second before responding, "I'm fine. How about you?"

"I'm okay. Have you talked to Bailey?"

"Yeah. She's feeling a lot better."

"I'm glad that she left town," Zoe said. "I can't believe what the media has been saying about her, and I told them so."

"We're pretty sure it was the janitor. On the surveillance video, he pulled something out of his pocket—probably his cell phone—and snapped the picture of them getting Bailey out of that closet. He's been let go, from what I've been told."

"I'm really sorry your family has to go through something like this."

"We'll be okay," Kyle assured her. "Zoe, I know I've been acting kind of weird lately, and I want to apologize."

"I know that you're worried about your family."

"Thank you for being here for me. I want you to know that I appreciate it."

Zoe frowned. "Kyle, what is this really about?"

"I know that you aren't sure of my feelings for you, but I would like a chance to prove myself to you."

"How do you intend to do that?" Zoe asked.

"I figure we could get things jumping by taking a private swing-dance lesson. I don't know about you, but I've always wanted to learn the Lindy Hop."

She laughed. "Are you serious?"

"Yeah. I remember you once talking about how much you loved the dances they did in the '30s. I thought this would be a perfect way to really get to know each other."

"That conversation happened over three or four years ago, Kyle." Zoe was touched that he remembered, although she cursed her weakness. Once again, she was caving where Kyle Hamilton was concerned. But she just couldn't help herself. "I have to admit, I'm curious to see you doing the Lindy Hop."

"So is it a date?" he asked.

"Yes. It's a date."

After they hung up, Zoe could not concentrate on her work. She cautioned herself to keep her feelings under wraps. She would accept what Kyle offered at face value—she would not look for anything more than he was willing to give. However, it touched her deeply that he had remembered about the swing dancing. It was a very sweet gesture.

Chapter 15

"Okay, face Zoe and position your left arm," the dance instructor told Kyle. "Very good…now make sure that your hand is at her waist."

Zoe met his gaze and grinned. "Having fun yet?"

"I am," Kyle said with a smile. He had hoped taking a dance lesson would be a good idea and he was pleasantly surprised to find that it was. Zoe looked as though she was having a wonderful time.

"Now bring your arm with you, which will pull her toward you."

He glanced over at the instructor and her dance partner and imitated what they were doing.

Her eyes flashed to his. "That was so much fun," Zoe told him after the class ended.

He savored the feel of her in his arms. To Kyle, it felt as if he'd come home—there was no other way to explain it.

"I wouldn't mind taking another lesson," he said.

She offered an easy smile. "Really?"

Kyle nodded. "I enjoyed it."

She smiled up at him and he had to resist the urge to kiss her right then and there. He reminded himself that he was taking it slowly with her as he evaluated the situation.

"Can we do it again?" she asked.

"Sure."

"I really like this side of you, Kyle."

He smiled. "I'm glad."

For a moment, Kyle saw a flash of uncertainty on Zoe's face, and he wondered if Zoe could read him so well that she could sense his doubt.

The thought unnerved him.

"You look like you had a good time," Liora commented when Zoe entered their apartment.

"I did," Zoe said with a grin. "Kyle and I had a private dance lesson. We learned how to do the Lindy Hop."

"Really? How did it go?"

She laughed. "We realized that the Lindy Hop is not a dance we can learn with just one lesson. We're going to have a few more sessions."

"I never would've thought a man like Kyle Hamilton would do something like that. He must really be crazy about you."

"I'm sure he did it just to get my attention, Liora. I have to admit that it worked like a charm."

"Are you going out with him again?"

Zoe nodded. "I must be out of my mind, huh?"

"No, I don't think so. I think you and Kyle need to see where this goes. It's obvious that you two care for each other. Just have fun, Zoe."

"I'm not sure what Kyle really wants, but I'm not going to worry about it," she said. "I'm just going to take this one day at a time and enjoy the ride."

Zoe had asked Kyle to meet her at her favorite indie bookstore. Kyle walked inside and glanced around at the rare and vintage photography books, looking for her.

"Thanks for meeting me here," Zoe said. "I love to come here for inspiration." She wanted to share this special place with him.

Kyle picked up a book. "*New York Sex, 1979–1985.* Interesting."

She laughed. "Out of all of the books in the bookstore, you *would* find that one interesting."

"It aroused my curiosity," he murmured as he turned the pages.

Zoe glanced over to peer at the page he was

reading. Heat rose to her face. The image was a vivid reminder of what had happened between them in the supply room.

He glanced in her direction.

She cleared her throat noisily. "I can't believe you're still holding that book."

Kyle gave her a mischievous grin. "I think I'm going to buy it. It's given me a lot of inspiration."

"Keep your voice down," she whispered.

He burst into laughter. "You're actually blushing."

She gave him a playful punch on the arm. "I think we should go over there and check out those books."

"What kind are they?" Kyle wanted to know.

"Religious books. I'm sure we can find a couple of bibles."

They both laughed.

"I was thinking that we could have dinner at Jason's Kitchen and Wine Bar."

"Sounds good," Zoe said.

They left the bookstore forty-five minutes later.

"We'd like to be seated in the back of the dining room," Kyle told the maître d'. Zoe glanced at him, clearly picking up on the fact that he wanted to sit in the more intimate section of the restaurant.

A round of laughter sounded from a nearby table. She gave him a tiny smile before saying, "Sounds like they're having a good time."

"Yeah," he agreed.

The waiter arrived and they ordered. Kyle noticed that Zoe looked strangely nervous. The depth of tenderness washing through him took his breath away. He had never been able to classify this thing he had for her. But now as his gaze locked on hers as he sat in the restaurant, the truth seemed so obvious he couldn't believe he'd so stupidly missed it.

He was in love with her.

Kyle wasn't sure how or when it had happened.

He sighed.

He never saw this coming.

And yet it made more sense than anything else in the whole world.

Zoe hummed softly as she removed her clothes and padded barefoot into the bath. Tonight couldn't have been more perfect.

She released a soft sigh of pleasure as the hot, soothing water ran down her body. Zoe closed her eyes as her tension melted away.

She could hear her cell phone ringing when she stepped out of the bath. Zoe quickly wrapped a fluffy towel around her and then ran to answer her phone.

By the time she got to the dresser, the caller had hung up.

It was an unidentified number.

Whoever it was did not bother to leave a voice message.

Zoe dried off and slipped into a pair of cotton pajama pants and a camisole top. She climbed into her bed and pulled out her iPad to go over her calendar. Jerry had called a meeting for ten in the morning. *Good, I can sleep in tomorrow,* she thought to herself.

She glanced over at the sketch pad on her nightstand. Zoe loved all of her designs, but these were not for Guava and not for those who could afford haute-couture fashions. She remembered all too well what it was like to grow up without the money to spend on the styles of clothing she wanted to wear. Zoe had eventually begun sewing her own outfits. She was able to earn money by making clothes for her friends, as well.

It had always been a dream of hers to create a collection of affordable fashions. Zoe hoped to one day have her own label, but that would never happen as long as she stayed with Guava. For now Zoe was content—she was not looking to leave. However, if the opportunity ever offered itself… she would leave Guava and strike out on her own.

"Where's Zoe?" Jerry inquired when Sasha strolled into his office. "Did you tell her that the meeting was moved up an hour?"

"I called her at home last night and left a message," Sasha said smoothly. In truth, Sasha had called Zoe's cell phone...but did not leave a message. She'd never had any intention of leaving a message, actually.

"Then why isn't she here?"

"I don't know," Sasha replied. She handed him her phone. "See, I called her right after I talked to you." Zoe's number was in her call log—solid proof that no one could refute. "She's probably somewhere with Kyle," Sasha announced. "I told you that she couldn't be trusted. Zoe and Kyle have gotten pretty close, in case you haven't noticed."

"Yes, Sasha, I've noticed, thank you," Jerry said caustically.

Sasha gave him a smug look. "She's been spending a lot of time with him. I heard her on the phone making plans for dinner yesterday. I think she's getting ready to jump ship and go back to RHD."

"I've had it with Kyle Hamilton," Jerry said. "He'll do whatever he can to try to convince her to return to RHD, but Zoe's too smart for that. You're wrong, Sasha. Zoe would never leave Guava."

Jerry's words angered Sasha. She was sick and tired of him defending Zoe. "Women will do anything for love. Zoe's feelings for Kyle can only mean trouble for us—unless you get rid of her."

He shook his head. "We need her, Sasha."

"For what?" she questioned. "We have other designers with talent."

"None come close to Zoe. Myself included. We have no chance of a real collection without Zoe." Jerry's hands curled into fists.

"We don't need her, Jerry," Sasha insisted.

Jerry didn't seem to hear her. He met Sasha's gaze. "I need you to do something for me."

"What is it?"

"Right now there is a lot of attention on Bailey Hamilton. We need to change the focus."

Sasha gave Jerry a delighted grin. "Exactly what did you have in mind?"

The meeting was in full swing by the time Zoe arrived. Confused, she eased into the conference room and dropped down into an empty chair.

"Zoe, I'm glad you finally decided to grace us with your presence," Jerry said.

"I thought the meeting was at ten," she said. "I wasn't aware that the time had changed."

She glanced at Sasha, remembered the phone call from the night before and knew instantly what had happened.

Sasha was supposed to let her know of the time change but had conveniently not left her a message.

After the meeting, Zoe walked up to Jerry and said, "I'm sorry for being late. I would've been here if I'd known about the change in time."

"Sasha called you last night and left you a message."

Zoe gave Jerry a look. "She may have called, but she didn't leave a message."

"I don't understand why she'd call you and not leave a message," he said. "That just doesn't make sense."

"Jerry, I received a called from a blocked number and no message was left. I have no reason to lie."

"How was dinner with Kyle?" he asked.

"Excuse me?"

"Your dinner with Kyle. How was it?"

Zoe folded her arms. "How do you know Kyle and I had dinner?"

"I hear that you two are a couple now."

Zoe refused to say a word.

"He's just using you, Zoe. I hope that you know that."

"Jerry, I'm not about to have this discussion with you."

"I don't want to see you get hurt."

Zoe, furious, turned on her heel and went in search of Sasha.

"I'm tired of the childish games, Sasha," Zoe said when she confronted the woman in the break room. "What have I done to you?"

"You exist," she said coolly.

"And you're going to have to get over it. Face it, Sasha. I'm not going anywhere."

"I don't know. You keep missing important meetings or appointments."

"You are sorely testing me," Zoe warned.

"Poor Zoe," Sasha cooed sarcastically. "I guess we'll just have to see what happens."

Chapter 16

Sasha trembled with anger as she walked away from Zoe.

Everyone thought Zoe was sweet and innocent, but she knew better. Sasha knew that Zoe was only at Guava until she could get a better offer—she had no company loyalty. If she did, then she would not be associating with the likes of Kyle Hamilton.

How could Jerry put up with this? If it were me, I would have fired Zoe a long time ago.

He was probably blinded by his infatuation.

Whenever Sasha mentioned his feelings for Zoe, Jerry would deny them, but she wasn't a fool. She saw the way he looked at her. Everyone did.

It was the same way that he used to look at

Sasha. Although Jerry had kicked her to the curb, she was still very loyal to him. She had a plan for her future and she knew that he could help her achieve her goals—it was why she put up with him.

A small part of her loved Jerry and it bothered her to see him fawn over Zoe. Sasha was not delusional, though. She knew that Jerry loved himself more than anyone else in the world. She could deal with that. But she could not deal with Zoe Sinclair taking up all the glory.

It was time someone put the witch in her place.

Sasha burst into Jerry's office. "We need to talk. I've had a change of heart."

She had no defense against him.

Although she braced herself against his magnetism, Zoe never stood a chance. They were seated across from each other in one of Kyle's favorite eateries.

A waiter approached with a bottle of wine nestled inside a gleaming silver bucket.

Zoe bit her lip as the waiter poured a sip of wine into a glass and presented it to Kyle for tasting.

He nodded in approval.

Once the waiter disappeared, Zoe reached for her glass and took a sip, hoping to ease the sudden dryness in her throat.

Kyle's chocolate-brown eyes narrowed on her

and he picked up his glass. Watching her over the rim, he swallowed, and then set the glass back onto the table.

Soon another waiter appeared, this time delivering a dinner that Kyle had clearly ordered earlier.

Surprised, Zoe looked down at the serving of chicken breast and fettuccine in mushroom sauce before lifting her gaze to his in question.

"I remembered you liked it," he said.

What was she supposed to do with that? she wondered. Kyle actually remembered more than five years later what her favorite foods were? Why? Why would he recall something so small?

He smiled faintly, laid his napkin across his lap and, picking up his knife and fork, sliced into his filet mignon.

"You have a good memory." She took a bite of her dinner and smiled. It was cooked to perfection.

"I remember everything about you, Zoe."

She glanced around the room. This was her first time at the Diamond Club. While they dined, a jazz band performed in the background. "This is as lovely as I thought it would be," Zoe commented.

"It's one of my favorite places," Kyle said. "I used to come here a lot, but it's been a while."

"You are very different from the man I imagined you to be." She wiped her mouth on the edge of her napkin.

"I hope that's a good thing."

She smiled. "It is. I used to think that you were exactly the kind of man my mother warned me about. She would like you, Kyle. I've also discovered that you're not as self-absorbed as people seem to think."

He laughed. "Shhh...don't tell anybody."

After they finished their dinner, Kyle drove her home.

Zoe still was not completely convinced that he was not trying to manipulate her, despite the fact that he had behaved like a perfect gentleman all evening. But when they arrived at her apartment, she asked, "Would you like to come in for a while?"

"I'd love to," he said, his husky voice sending chills down her spine.

They settled down in the living room.

"I really like you, Zoe. I want to see where this is going." He reached over and took her hand in his.

"Are you saying that you want a relationship?" Zoe asked. She needed to be sure that she was hearing him correctly.

He pulled her closer to him.

Her lips parted in protest, but before she could utter a word, Kyle closed the distance between them without hesitation.

He took her mouth as if it was his to do with as he pleased, making it his own in a way that had

Zoe's hands rising of their own volition, her fingers curling into his shirt. Her moan slid free of her mouth and into Kyle's.

The kiss was explosive, consuming and intense.

All Zoe could think about was the heat of Kyle's body as he pulled her closer. She might regret this tomorrow, but she just wasn't strong enough to walk away tonight.

Kyle released Zoe slowly, leaving her breathless, hungry for more of his kisses and drowning in desire.

She gazed into his chocolate-brown eyes.

"You are irresistible," he murmured, as though he had reached some internal understanding with himself. Kyle lowered his head to hers and pressed a single kiss on her lips.

"I think we…um…need to stop." Zoe cleared her throat quietly. "I just need…"

"Give us a chance," he whispered. "I know that you care for me. I feel the same way about you, Zoe."

She looked into his eyes and what she glimpsed in their depths spoke volumes.

"Okay," she whispered. "However, there is one ground rule. I'm not going to have sex with you again until I feel we are both ready to take our relationship to the next level."

"I can live with that," Kyle said. "I'll be taking a lot of cold showers, but I can manage."

Although she was trying hard not to fall deeper and deeper in love with him, Zoe was failing over and over again.

It had been a struggle to not blurt it out to Kyle, but Zoe wasn't sure that it was something he was ready to hear.

After dinner, they walked out to the car.

Kyle muttered a curse when he looked down at his tires. All four had been slashed.

"I don't think someone is after Bailey," Zoe said as she looked down at Kyle's slashed tires. "Kyle, I think your whole family may be in danger."

"This may have just been some kids."

She shook her head. "Think about it, Kyle. Someone locked us in a closet, and then kidnapped Bailey. Now your tires have been slashed. . . ."

"Someone is trying to send my family a message," he agreed. "But who could have it in for us like this?"

"I don't know," Zoe said. "But you're a high-profile family and there's a lot of jealousy out there. Now, if it were my car, I would know exactly who was to blame."

"Why do you say that?" he asked.

"Because there's this woman at Guava who's made it clear that she hates the very air I breathe."

"Really?"

Zoe nodded. "At least she's let me know it. But

you don't have any idea who is behind all this stuff. Kyle, you really need to be careful. All of you."

"I don't want to worry my parents with this."

"You're going to have to tell them. They need to be able to protect themselves from whoever is out there." She reached over and covered his hand with her own. "I hate to see you going through something like this."

"My family has never experienced anyone trying to bring harm to us. I feel helpless because I don't have a clue as to where to find this person or persons."

"I don't think you'll have to look too far, Kyle. You just need to be aware of your surroundings and of the people around you."

He turned to her with a strange look on her face. "Does that include you?" he questioned.

She was stunned by his words. "No, it doesn't. Kyle, you can trust me."

He did not respond.

Zoe felt sick to her stomach. After the conversation they'd had earlier, after what she'd been about to tell him, she couldn't believe her ears.

Kyle was suspicious of her.

"Kyle, I think you should see this," Nelson said from the doorway of Kyle's office.

"What is it?" he asked as he pushed away

from his desk and followed Nelson down to the mail room.

"This is the new shipment of fabric you've been expecting," Nelson explained as he lifted the flap open.

Kyle could not believe his eyes. "Was the box sealed when it arrived?"

The mail staff nodded.

"It looks like someone intentionally slashed up the fabric."

Nelson agreed. "I called the supplier and they are sending out a replacement. They said it was not in that condition when it left the manufacturer, however."

"I'm sure of that," Kyle said. "We've had a long relationship with this particular company."

"This is really strange," Nelson muttered.

Kyle gestured for his cousin to follow him into the hallway. He waited until he could not be overheard. "It's not that strange. Someone is out to destroy RHD. My tires were slashed the other night."

"Do you have any idea who's doing this?"

"No," he said. "Not yet, but I intend to find out if it's the last thing I ever do."

Kyle picked up his telephone and dialed Zoe's number as soon as he reached his office.

"Hey, it's me," he told her. "Do you have about an hour or two free in your schedule today?"

"Yes," she said. "What's up?"

"Can you meet me at my place around one?" Kyle asked. He wanted to talk to her face-to-face. He wanted there to be no misunderstandings between them.

"I'll be there."

Kyle left the office, but not before telling Nelson, "I'm leaving for a couple of hours. I'll be at the apartment if you need me."

"Should I mention the shipment to your father?"

"No, I'll tell him."

When Zoe arrived at the apartment, she took one look at Kyle's face and said, "Kyle, what's wrong?"

"One of our fabric shipments arrived earlier. It was shredded."

She gasped in surprise. "Are you serious?"

"Yeah," he said. "I wish I wasn't."

"Kyle, I'm so sorry. I can't believe this."

"I think that you're right about the incidents all being related," Kyle told her. "Someone is definitely trying to sabotage RHD and ruin my family. I'm not about to let that happen."

"This is getting scary."

"Zoe, I care for you and I don't want you getting caught up in this. I think we need to keep our distance so that you don't end up as collateral damage."

"Do you think that this person will try to come after me?"

"Not if you stay away from me."

"You need to tell the police about this," Zoe urged.

"Tell them what?" Kyle demanded. "We don't know who is after us."

"You can tell them about all of the incidents. They will be able to find the people responsible."

"We need to stay away from each other," Kyle repeated.

"I have to be honest with you. I don't think your wanting me out of your life has anything to do with what's been going on."

He looked confused. "What are you talking about, Zoe?"

"I'm sure you know what I mean," she said, a little too quietly.

Kyle shook his head. "No, actually, I don't."

"What you refuse to say is that you and I are not on the same page when it comes to relationships," Zoe said. "I made it perfectly clear that I'm not looking for anything casual. You don't have to worry, Kyle. I've been through this with you, remember?" She picked up her purse and headed to the door. "I hope you find out who is after your family."

Before she knew it, Kyle's strong hands were turning her around, gripping her tight. "You're wrong. I don't think you understand at all."

Zoe looked away from him. She didn't want

to stumble further into the intensity of his brown eyes. "I think I understand completely. Kyle, there is nothing meaningful between us. We have no potential. I think it's best if we just stop seeing each other."

"Wait a minute, Zoe," he called out. "Hey, you've got this completely wrong. I just don't want anything to happen to you because of me."

She wore an expression of disbelief.

"I'm telling you the truth," Kyle said. "Why is it so hard to believe me?"

"Did you seriously just ask me that question? I guess you've forgotten what happened all those years ago."

"Let's talk about it."

She shook her head. "You've got a lot going on, Kyle. I don't want to add to it."

"No. We need to have this conversation."

"Why?" Zoe demanded.

Seconds passed and then finally the breath Kyle had been trying to contain shot past his throat with the only answer he had. "I was scared by what I felt for you, Zoe," he confessed, "and I was also threatened by your raw talent. I was working to make a name for myself and then you walked into RHD. My father was raving about your work."

She blinked, as shocked by the break in his demeanor as he was. "I was there to learn from you. I wanted you to be my mentor, Kyle."

"I understand that now," he said. "I realize just how immature I was back then. I'm sorry, Zoe. My focus has always been on making my father proud."

"I know that," Zoe murmured. "I just never understood why you couldn't see that he was already proud of you, Kyle."

"He demanded excellence from everyone, and he's a hard man to work for at times."

She smiled. "You have the same work ethic."

"Yeah, I guess I do."

"Kyle, I know that you aren't the type of man who wants a wife and children. I understand this, but I need you to respect that I am not the type of woman who wants to be single for the rest of her life. I want to get married and I want children." She held up her hands helplessly, pain glittering in her eyes. "This is never going to work."

"I'm not ready to give up on us," he countered.

"Kyle, I need some time to really think about everything."

"You're running away," he accused.

"No, I'm giving you the space you need to really figure out what you want from me." Zoe headed to the door with a heavy heart. Before she left, she looked back at him and fought tears as best she could. "Be safe."

"I saw Kyle today," Zoe announced as she handed Liora a plate laden with grilled chicken, broccoli and a whole-wheat dinner roll.

"Sounds like you two are getting close."

Zoe followed Liora to the dinner table and sat down. "We had an honest conversation and I'm convinced that he's not really ready for a relationship. He kept telling me that we need to stay away from each other because he wants to keep me safe. It looks like someone is trying to sabotage RHD."

"It is very possible that he wants you, but that he's really worried about your safety."

"Liora, I don't think that's true," she said. "Nobody has bothered me, and Kyle and I have spent a lot of time together. This is just an excuse to keep me at a distance."

"With all the crazy stuff that's been happening with that family, I don't really blame him, Zoe."

"I don't know," she said.

"Why are you so afraid to give Kyle a chance?" Liora asked. "I know that you're in love with him."

She looked over at her roommate. "I do love Kyle, but I don't want my heart broken."

"You can't be afraid to take a chance on love."

"I don't mind taking a chance on love—it's Kyle that I'm not so sure about," Zoe confessed.

Liora stayed silent, leaving Zoe's words echoing in her own ears.

Chapter 17

Zoe had given Kyle much to think about. The truth of the matter was that he did not want to lose her. He was in love with her. Kyle had no idea when it had happened, but it did not really matter. She was the woman he wanted to spend the rest of his life with. The question was, what would happen if he told her?

"You look like you're in deep thought," Nelson said.

"I was thinking about Zoe," Kyle confessed. "I'm in love with her."

"You're just realizing this?"

"Yeah."

"I knew it the moment I saw how you reacted when you thought she was interested in me."

Kyle smiled a little. “I can’t see my life without her in it. Nelson, this is crazy. I’ve never felt this way about any woman.”

Nelson chuckled. “So what are you going to do about it?”

“Zoe thinks that I only want a casual relationship with her, but that’s not true. I’m going to have to find a way to convince Zoe that I want her to be a part of my life.”

“You don’t think she’ll believe you?”

“I don’t know,” he admitted. “Things have been strained between us lately—mostly due to me, I’m sure—but I intend to fix it.”

He could change her mind. Zoe wasn’t immune to him—her response to him had been real and unfeigned. A physical reaction was one thing, but the softening of her heart to him—that was something else entirely.

“It won’t be too hard,” Nelson said. “Zoe is in love with you.”

“I’m not so sure,” Kyle countered. He rubbed a hand across his chest but couldn’t massage away the heartache there at the thought of losing her. In a very short time, he had become addicted to Zoe’s presence, her spirit and her incredible smiles.

“Have you considered telling her what you just told me?”

“What? That I’m in love with her?”

Nelson nodded with a big grin on his face. "The ball is in your court, cousin."

The desperate need to distract herself from unwelcome thoughts of Kyle threatened to overtake Zoe. She had cleaned her apartment from top to bottom and spent hours with different projects to keep her mind off him.

She hated to admit it, but nothing worked.

"Knock, knock...."

Zoe looked up from her desk. Her heart stopped at the sight of Kyle in her office. "Kyle, what are you doing here?"

"I wanted to talk to you," he replied. "It won't take long."

"Is something wrong?" She could not imagine what would bring him to Guava. But whatever it was, it must be bad news.

Zoe rose to her feet and walked around her desk. "Is everything okay?"

"Everything is fine," he said.

"Then let's get out of here. If Jerry sees you, he'll have a fit."

She rushed him into the elevator, praying that none of the staff members noticed him. "Why on earth did you come here?"

"I just wanted to tell you face-to-face that I'm not giving up on us. Zoe, I know that I've messed up in the past, but things are different now."

"Kyle, you didn't have to come all the way here to tell me this."

"You needed to see my face so you would know that I was telling the truth."

"I don't have time to have this conversation right now," she said softly.

"Will you please come to my place after work? I really want to talk to you."

"I'll call you later," she promised.

"Zoe, please give me a chance to make this right between us."

She stole a quick peek at a clock hanging on the wall in the reception area. "I'll call you and let you know if I can make it."

Kyle kissed her and then left.

After her meeting, Zoe waited until it was almost time for her to leave the office before calling Kyle.

"I wasn't sure you were going to call me."

"I told you I would." No need to tell him that she almost didn't call him. She had gone back and forth most of the afternoon about it.

"I hope you're calling to tell me that I'll be seeing you later tonight," he said.

"I'm not sure it's a good idea."

"Why not?" Kyle asked.

"We don't want the same things."

"You don't know that."

"C'mon, Kyle, you are not ready for a serious relationship."

"Zoe, I want to be with you. Just give me a chance to prove it to you."

"We're very attracted to each other, Kyle, but there has to be more than just that physical attraction."

"I agree."

"If you're serious about me, Kyle, you'll find a way to prove it to me."

The next day, Zoe smiled as she read the card from Kyle. She glanced at her watch and said, "I need to get dressed."

She threw on a pair of jeans and a T-shirt under a military-style jacket. "Kyle Hamilton, what are you up to?" she whispered as she checked her reflection in the full-length mirror of her bedroom.

Downstairs, a limo was waiting for her.

Zoe had no idea where she was going, but Kyle's note had intrigued her. She was mildly surprised when the limo pulled up in front of a spa.

She made her way through the double doors, expecting to see him. Instead, she found that he had arranged for her to have a full-body massage, facial, manicure and pedicure.

From there, Zoe was whisked away to have her hair washed and styled, and a makeup artist applied the finishing touches.

The driver handed Zoe another card when she approached the limo.

"I guess this is our next stop," she said with a smile. "The Savonna Boutique."

"Mr. Hamilton designed this dress exclusively for you and he would like for you to wear it this evening," the manager told her when she arrived.

Zoe's eyes grew wide with surprise. "This is stunning."

The woman smiled and nodded in agreement.

"What is going on?" she asked herself, keenly aware of the futility of the question. Zoe was pretty sure that she was meeting Kyle somewhere, but she had no idea where. She had tried to pry information from the driver earlier but had not been successful.

She ran her fingers through her hair, fluffing up the curls.

Ready or not, here I come.

When the limo stopped in front of Lincoln Center, Zoe was confused until she saw Kyle. He was dressed in a tuxedo and looked extremely handsome.

She stepped out of the limo, dressed in the metallic-silver dress that left her toned legs on perfect display. "I was told that I have you to thank for this," Zoe said with a smile.

She shifted under his scrutiny, smoothing her hands over her hips with downward strokes.

He stared into her eyes a long moment, the muscles of his throat working as though he was trying to speak but somehow couldn't. "Zoe, you look beautiful," he finally managed.

Moonlight danced on the surface of the water in the fountain, gleaming brightly and reflecting off her dress. "I love this dress. The cut of the back and the line of the waist… It's gorgeous, Kyle."

"You were my inspiration."

It was then that she noticed that Kyle had arranged to have a table set up in front of the fountain, complete with candles, champagne and lobster. "You did all this for me?"

He nodded as he pulled out a chair for her. "I wanted tonight to be perfect."

She noticed two men standing nearby. "Who are they?"

"They will make sure that we're not disturbed."

Zoe fought back tears. No one had ever done anything like this for her. "This is incredible, Kyle."

"I'm glad you're pleased," he said.

For a moment they just stood there, and then he said, "I tried to get you out of my mind, tried to forget you, but it was no good. What I've come to realize is that I can't envision my life without you in it. I want something more. I love you, Zoe."

She was getting lost in his eyes, feeling herself

drawn closer and closer. Zoe struggled to maintain some control over her emotions. "Kyle—"

"Please hear me out," he pleaded. "I've loved you from the moment we met, but I didn't think I had any room in my life for a serious relationship." Kyle paused for a brief moment before continuing, "I want you more than I've ever wanted any woman in my life. Zoe, you're in my blood, my soul, my bones. I go to bed at night wanting you and I spend each and every day wanting you."

Zoe gazed at him, her emotions a wild, raging river inside her. Desire coursed through her veins and her heart filled with love. But opening her heart and soul to Kyle seemed far more risky than anything she had ever done in her life.

Kyle gazed at her, emotion burning behind his eyes. "I have never been a man to beg, but if I have to beg, I will, because you are my life."

Zoe eyed him, her thoughts whirling. A bright and hopeful joy fluttered inside her like a trapped bird trying to break free, but she was afraid to let it go.

She was afraid to let herself trust completely.

"Say something," he said after her silence dragged on.

"I…I want a husband and a family. I want a man who loves me."

A muscle tightened in his jaw; he wrapped his

arms around her shoulders and pulled her closer to him.

"I love you and I want you to be my wife. You only have to walk into a room and everything else fades away completely. If you want I'll stand up here on this fountain and shout it at the top of my lungs."

Before Zoe could respond, Kyle stepped up and began yelling, "I love this woman over here and I want the world to know."

She laughed. "Get down before you fall into the water."

He shook his head. "Not until you believe me."

His words resonated deep in Zoe's heart. "Kyle, I believe you. Now get down from there."

He did as she told him. "I'm not sure you are totally convinced, sweetheart. I feel like I need to provide further proof."

Kyle reached inside his jacket and pulled out a tiny red box. He opened it to reveal a diamond engagement ring. "Zoe, will you marry me?"

She swallowed hard and a single tear rolled down her cheek. "I love you," she murmured. "It's not easy for me to tell you this, but there it is—I love you, Kyle Hamilton, and yes, I'll marry you."

He placed the ring on her finger.

Zoe wiped away her tears. "I can't believe this is happening. I never expected that this evening would end with our getting engaged."

They kissed until Zoe's thoughts were a hazy blur of hunger and need. She couldn't think of anything but Kyle.

They parted some at the sound of applause from strangers all around them. Kyle kissed her again as some took pictures of the couple.

"I think we should take this back to my place," he said after a moment.

Zoe couldn't agree more.

As soon they arrived at his apartment, Kyle picked her up and carried her into his bedroom. He removed her shoes and gently laid her on the wide chaise in his bedroom.

She sighed with relief when he shifted her beside him and freed her of the dress he'd designed just for her. Zoe couldn't hold back a shiver at the torrent of sensation pouring through her.

He paused, concern on his face. "Are you cold?"

"No," she murmured. "Everything is perfect."

Zoe reached for his face and drew him down to her, kissing him fiercely. Kyle groaned and responded with the same hunger, his mouth tangling with hers, his hands exploring her curves.

"Do you have any idea just how much you mean to me?"

"Show me," she murmured.

Desire blazed in his eyes. Desire for her.

Zoe wanted this man who had poured out his heart to her in front of the fountain at Lincoln

Center. The man who was willing to shout it to the world.

She clutched him, pressing close even as Kyle pulled her closer still.

It wasn't enough for either of them.

"I love you so much," he managed between breaths.

Zoe's body was on fire. Heart racing, breath ragged, she couldn't think of anything other being with this amazing man—her soul mate.

"I was thinking we should get married as soon as possible," Kyle said on Sunday afternoon while they were getting dressed. He had invited Zoe to join his family for dinner.

"Maybe we should wait until we find out who's trying to sabotage your family," she suggested. "We don't want your family to be in the press any more than you have to be."

When they walked out of the bedroom and joined Nelson in the den, he said, "I wondered if you two were going to spend the day in bed."

Zoe blushed while Kyle chuckled.

"Come here and let me see that ring up close," Nelson demanded. "Let me pull out my sunglasses."

Grinning, she walked over to show off her sparkly diamond. "Your cousin has exquisite taste."

"Yes, he does," Nelson said. "I guess I need to find an apartment soon."

"You don't have to move," Zoe and Kyle said in unison.

Nelson shook his head. "Actually, I can move into my mom's place. She wants to spend more time with me. I'd like to stay on with you as your assistant, Kyle. That is, if you still need someone."

"I do," he confirmed. "I'd love to keep you on."

Ten minutes later, they all headed to Roger and Lila's apartment.

Daniel and Brianna were already there when they arrived.

Lila greeted Zoe with a hug. "Oh, honey, I'm so glad to see you. I'm glad Kyle invited you to have dinner with us."

"I didn't just invite her to dinner, Mom," Kyle interjected. "I asked Zoe to become a permanent part of our family."

"Oh my goodness," Lila said as her eyes grew wet.

Brianna embraced Zoe. "I'm so happy for you and Kyle. Congratulations."

Roger hugged her next. "I wondered how long it would take my son to come to his senses. Better late than never, I guess."

Zoe laughed. "He wasn't the only one who needed to come to their senses. I'm just as guilty as he is."

"So have you set a wedding date?" Lila inquired.

"Not yet," Kyle said.

In the dining room, she sat down in the chair next to Kyle while Nelson sat on the other side of her. The only person missing was Bailey.

"I'm thrilled that you will soon be a part of this family," Lila said. "I've always believed that you were the one woman for Kyle."

Zoe grinned. "So did I."

After dinner, she offered to help clean up, but Lila and Brianna refused her assistance.

Zoe realized that she hadn't checked her voice mail all weekend and said to Kyle, "I'll be right back. I need to check my messages."

"Okay, sweetheart. Why don't you go into the office so that you're not disturbed?"

"I won't be long," she told him.

Zoe listened to her messages, but only one stood out for her. She giggled in excitement and rushed out of the office to tell Kyle.

Bailey was on speakerphone when she returned to the den. It was clear that she had just been told about their engagement.

"Where's Zoe? Is she there?"

"I'm here, Bailey."

"We're going to be sisters," she screamed through the phone, sparking laughter from everyone.

"Yes, we are," Zoe confirmed.

"I just want to know what took you two so long to get together."

She glanced over at Kyle and then said, "It doesn't matter. We're together now and it's for life."

"I'm so happy for you."

"Thank you, Bailey," Zoe said.

"I miss you all so much. I'm ready to come home."

"Honey, I want you to wait a little while longer," Roger said. "We'll bring you home as soon as we know something. We miss you, too."

Zoe knew that they had not told her about the other incidents, and that it seemed as if the entire family was the target. They didn't want to worry Bailey. She worried for all of them. Brianna and Lila never left home without a plainclothes bodyguard now. She was relieved that they seemed to be taking the unknown threat seriously.

When they got back to the apartment, Zoe couldn't contain herself any longer.

"Why are you grinning like that?" Kyle asked her. "Did you get some good news or something?"

"Actually, I did," she said. "I have an opportunity to have my own label and market it on the Fashion Network."

"Are you serious?"

She nodded. "This is something that I've always wanted, Kyle. I have dreamed of designing clothes that normal people can afford. They won't have to sacrifice fashion and style just because they can't afford to shop at Saks or a couture boutique."

"I'm happy for you, Zoe."

She met his gaze. "Do you really mean it?"

"Yeah, I do," he said. "Honey, I'm so proud of you."

"I love you."

"I love you, too."

"So when are you going to tell Jerry?" Kyle inquired.

"The sooner the better," she answered. "He's not going to like it one way or the other, but this is my dream."

"Do you want me with you when you tell him?"

Zoe shook her head. "Jerry is harmless, Kyle. His bark is definitely worse than his bite." She broke into a short laugh. "I'm getting married to the man of my dreams and I'm going to have my own fashion line."

Kyle chuckled. "I never thought I would be this happy at the thought of settling down, but I'm actually looking forward to being your husband."

"You do know that forever is a long time?"

"When it comes to you, baby, forever isn't near enough time."

Zoe knocked softly on the door to Jerry's office before sticking her head inside. "Do you have a few minutes to talk?"

"Sure," he said with a smile. "I always have time for my star designer."

She sat down in one of the chairs facing him. "Jerry, I really want to thank you for everything that you've done for me. I really appreciate you."

"Hey, what's this about?" he asked, his smile waning. "You sound like you're about to say good-bye."

Zoe met his gaze. "I am," she said softly.

He slammed his fist on the desk, causing her to jump at the sound. "I knew it. I knew Kyle Hamilton was going to try to steal you away, but I actually believed that you were more loyal than this. Sasha called this one right."

Zoe struggled to keep her anger in check at the mention of Sasha's name. "Kyle has nothing to do with my decision to leave Guava, Jerry. I was offered a chance to have my own label on the Fashion Network. I'm going to have my own show."

"What are you thinking, Zoe? You want to give up everything you've worked for at Guava for some lowbrow brand of clothing?"

"I don't expect you to understand my decision, Jerry. This is something I want to do. But I have to say, I thought you'd be happy for me."

"I would be if I thought you were making a smart decision."

"Excuse me?"

"Zoe, you are one of the lead designers at Guava.

Did you read the article in *Women's Wear Daily?* In the *New York Times?*"

"Jerry, this is my life."

His gaze traveled to her left hand. "And what is that on your finger?"

"I'm getting married. Kyle and I are engaged."

He was furious and did not bother to hide the fact. "I knew it."

"Jerry, you really need to get over this obsession you have with Kyle."

"You need to wise up, Zoe," he snapped in response. "Can't you see what he's doing? Kyle doesn't want you working at Guava."

Zoe rose to her feet. "I'll give you a formal written resignation letter before I leave today."

"Consider this your last day," Jerry said. "I'm sure you understand...trade secrets and all. Security will escort you out."

"How did things go with Jerry?" Kyle inquired when she returned to the apartment later.

"I've never seen him so angry," Zoe said. "He's morphed into someone I don't know."

"I'm sure he blamed me for your wanting to leave Guava."

"Yeah, he did. I told him that it had nothing to do with you, but then Jerry saw my engagement ring. It was all over then."

"He'll get over it," Kyle said.

"I feel bad, though. I thought he and I were friends."

"Jerry doesn't know what it means to be a friend, Zoe."

He pulled her into his arms. "I must confess that I'm glad you're no longer working with him. You don't need to deal with his insecurities on a daily basis. The man is talented, but he just doesn't believe in himself. He wants to blame everyone else when things don't go his way."

"Well, now we don't ever have to worry about Jerry again," Zoe murmured. "He'll find another designer to groom. I'll always be grateful to him for everything he taught me."

"I don't want to talk about Jerry Prentice anymore."

"What would you like to do?" she asked.

Leading her to the bedroom, he said, "I have a few ideas…."

Epilogue

The rainy night in New York was perfect for staying inside and enjoying a quiet dinner. Soft contemporary jazz floated through the apartment, accompanied by the soft patter of raindrops on the balcony.

The sound of footsteps echoed on the hardwood floors leading upstairs, dissolving into silence as the expensively clad feet landed on plush carpet, moving with purpose.

The door at the end of the second floor opened to reveal a room with photographs and newspaper clippings of the Hamilton family decorating the walls. Pictures of Roger and Lila at different events and venues were pinned up neatly. Below them, various photos of their children were plastered in place.

A gloved hand traced the outline of Bailey's face before moving on to a head shot of Brianna. The next photo, one of Kyle, captured and held the attention of the person gazing at the pictures. On the desk nearby, a scrapbook containing years of articles on the Hamilton family lay open. A stack of more recent photos lay beside a tabloid article of Bailey's disappearance.

Many years had gone into following this family—years of searching for skeletons in their closets. So far, there had been no success on that end. There had to be something to use against them, but nothing had been discovered yet.

"This is far from over. I'm not going to give up. I'm going to find a way to destroy all of the Hamiltons...by any means necessary."

* * * * *

A new miniseries featuring fan-favorite authors!

The Hamiltons: Fashioned with Love

Family. Glamour. Passion.

Jacquelin Thomas	Pamela Yaye	Farrah Rochon
Styles of Seduction	*Designed by Desire*	*Runaway Attraction*
Available September 2013	***Available October 2013***	***Available November 2013***

KPHFWLC13

Change is in the air…

Until Now

Part of the sizzling *Hart to Hart* miniseries!

USA TODAY
Bestselling Author

Kayla Perrin

With her abusive ex-husband in prison, Tamara Jackson has finally found peace. She pledges to remain strong, independent and single—then she meets sexy detective Marshall Jennings. His persistent pursuit soon has Tamara second-guessing her strategy. Passion quickly cascades into something more—a wave of emotions that may sweep them into everlasting love….

Available September 2013 wherever books are sold!

KPKP3200913